The Rome Express

The Rome Express, the *direttissimo*, or most direct, was approaching Paris one morning in March, when it became known to the occupants of the sleeping car that there was something amiss, very much amiss, in the car.

The train was traveling the last stage, between Laroche and Paris, a run of a hundred miles without a stop. It had halted at Laroche for early breakfast, and many, if not all the passengers, had turned out. Of those in the sleeping car, seven in number, six had been seen in the restaurant, or about the platform; the seventh, a lady, had not stirred. All had reentered their berths to sleep or doze when the train went on, but several were on the move as it neared Paris, taking their turn at the lavatory, calling for water, towels, making the usual stir of preparation as the end of a journey was at hand.

There were many calls for the porter, yet no porter appeared. At last the attendant was found–lazy villain! asleep, snoring loudly, stertorously, in his little bunk at the end of the car. He was roused with difficulty, and set about his work in a dull, unwilling, lethargic way, which promised badly for his tips from those he was supposed to serve.

By degrees all the passengers got dressed, all but two, the lady in 9 and 10, who had made no sign as yet; and the man who occupied alone a double berth next her, numbered 7 and 8.

As it was the porter's duty to call everyone, and as he was anxious, like the rest of his class, to get rid of his travelers as soon as possible after arrival, he rapped at each of the two closed doors behind which people presumably still slept, but there was no answer from No. 7 and 8.

Again and again the porter knocked and called loudly. Still meeting with no response, he opened the door of the compartment and went in.

It was now broad daylight. No blind was down; indeed, the one narrow window was open, wide; and the whole of the interior of the compartment was plainly visible, all and everything in it.

The occupant lay on his bed motionless. Sound asleep? No, not merely asleep–the twisted unnatural lie of the limbs, the contorted legs, the one arm drooping listlessly but stiffly over the side of the berth, told of a deeper, more eternal sleep.

The man was dead. Dead–and not from natural causes.

One glance at the blood stained bedclothes, one look at the gaping wound in the breast, at the battered, mangled face, told the terrible story.

It was murder! Murder most foul! The victim had been stabbed to the heart.

With a wild, affrighted, cry the porter rushed out of the compartment, and to the eager questioning of all who crowded round him, he could only mutter in confused and trembling accents:

"There! There! In there!"

Thus the fact of the murder became known to everyone by personal inspection, for everyone (even the lady had appeared for just a moment) had looked in where the body lay. The compartment was filled for some ten minutes or more by an excited, gesticulating, polyglot mob of half a dozen, all talking at once in French, English, and Italian.

The Rome Express

By Arthur Griffiths

Originally published in 1907

The Rome Express

© 2010 Resurrected Press

Published by Intrepid Ink, LLC

Intrepid Ink, LLC provides full publishing services to authors of fiction and non-fiction books, eBooks and websites. From editing to formatting, to publishing, to marketing, Intrepid Ink gets your creative works into the hands of the people who want to read them.
Find out more at www.IntrepidInk.com.

ISBN 10: 0-9843857-6-2
ISBN 13: 978-0-9843857-6-8

Printed in the United States of America

FOREWORD

The Rome Express, the very words conjure up a romantic time when travel, at least for those who could afford a compartment in a first class car, was elegant and refined. One could board the night train in Rome, dine along the way, sleep in comfortable accommodations and wake up at the station in Paris refreshed and ready to go.

In a scant half century railroads had covered the continent of Europe. Express lines connected the capitols and major cities covering distances in hours that would have taken days or weeks of arduous and dangerous travel by horse drawn coach before their advent. And it all ran like clockwork. One had only to consult one's copy of Bradshaw to find the schedules and connecting trains so that one could travel from anywhere to anywhere else with a minimum of fuss.

Train travel was indeed luxurious for those who had money, with sleeping cars, dining cars, smoking cars, stops at track side restaurants. First class passengers were shielded from the lower orders. Porters were available to provide services like hot water for washing, setting up the sleeping arrangements of the compartments, and making sure one was awake in time for arrival at the station.

This is the picture that Major Arthur Griffiths paints in "The Rome Express." Of course, not everything can be expected to run smoothly, especially when a body is discovered in one of the compartments. Then one must deal with officious foreign policemen and other inconveniences.

As a footnote, several films have been made based on the novel, "Rome Express" in 1932 and "Sleeping Car to Trieste" made after World War II.

About the Author

Major Arthur Griffiths (1838-1908) was born at an Indian garrison post, a descendent of a long line of military men. After serving as a Second Lieutenant during the Crimean War his regiment was posted to Halifax, Nova Scotia. He also served for a period at Gibraltar before retiring from the military to join the civil service where he held the post of Inspector of Prisons.

He wrote numerous books including *"Mysteries of Police and Crime"*, *"The Chronicles of Newgate"*, *"The Passenger from Calais"*, and *"The Rome Express."*

Greg Fowlkes
Editor-In-Chief
Resurrected Press

1

The Rome Express, the *direttissimo*, or most direct, was approaching Paris one morning in March, when it became known to the occupants of the sleeping-car that there was something amiss, very much amiss, in the car.

The train was travelling the last stage, between Laroche and Paris, a run of a hundred miles without a stop. It had halted at Laroche for early breakfast, and many, if not all the passengers, had turned out. Of those in the sleeping-car, seven in number, six had been seen in the restaurant, or about the platform; the seventh, a lady, had not stirred. All had reentered their berths to sleep or doze when the train went on, but several were on the move as it neared Paris, taking their turn at the lavatory, calling for water, towels, making the usual stir of preparation as the end of a journey was at hand.

There were many calls for the porter, yet no porter appeared. At last the attendant was found–lazy villain!–asleep, snoring loudly, stertorously, in his little bunk at the end of the car. He was roused with difficulty, and set about his work in a dull, unwilling, lethargic way, which promised badly for his tips from those he was supposed to serve.

By degrees all the passengers got dressed, all but two,–the lady in 9 and 10, who had made no sign as yet; and the man who occupied alone a double berth next her, numbered 7 and 8.

As it was the porter's duty to call everyone, and as he was anxious, like the rest of his class, to get rid of his travellers as soon as possible after arrival, he rapped at each of the two closed doors behind which people presumably still slept.

The lady cried "All right," but there was no answer from No. 7 and 8.

Again and again the porter knocked and called loudly. Still meeting with no response, he opened the door of the compartment and went in.

It was now broad daylight. No blind was down; indeed, the one narrow window was open, wide; and the whole of the interior of the compartment was plainly visible, all and everything in it.

The occupant lay on his bed motionless. Sound asleep? No, not merely asleep–the twisted unnatural lie of the limbs, the contorted legs, the one arm drooping listlessly but stiffly over the side of the berth, told of a deeper, more eternal sleep.

The man was dead. Dead–and not from natural causes.

One glance at the blood-stained bedclothes, one look at the gaping wound in the breast, at the battered, mangled face, told the terrible story.

It was murder! Murder most foul! The victim had been stabbed to the heart.

With a wild, affrighted, cry the porter rushed out of the compartment, and to the eager questioning of all who crowded round him, he could only mutter in confused and trembling accents:

"There! There! In there!"

Thus the fact of the murder became known to everyone by personal inspection, for everyone (even the lady had appeared for just a moment) had looked in where the body lay. The compartment was filled for some ten minutes or more by an excited, gesticulating, polyglot mob of half a dozen, all talking at once in French, English, and Italian.

The first attempt to restore order was made by a tall man, middle-aged, but erect in his bearing, with bright eyes and alert manner, who took the porter aside, and said sharply in good French, but with a strong English accent:

"Here! It's your business to do something. No one has any right to be in that compartment now. There may be reasons–traces–things to remove; never mind what. But get them all out. Be sharp about it; and lock the door. Remember you will be held responsible to justice."

The porter shuddered, so did many of the passengers who had overheard the Englishman's last words.

Justice! It is not to be trifled with anywhere, least of all in France, where the uncomfortable superstition prevails that everyone who can be reasonably suspected of a crime is held to be guilty of that crime until his innocence is clearly proved.

All those six passengers and the porter were now brought within the category of the accused. They were all open to suspicion; they, and they alone, for the murdered man had been seen alive at Laroche, and the fell deed must have been done since then, while the train was in transit, that is to say, going at express speed, when no one could leave it except at peril of his life.

"Deuced awkward for us!" said the tall English general, Sir Charles Collingham by name, to his brother the parson, when he had reentered their compartment and shut the door.

"I can't see it. In what way?" asked the Reverend Silas Collingham, a typical English cleric, with a rubicund face and square-cut white whiskers, dressed in a suit of black serge, and wearing the professional white tie.

"Why, we shall be detained, of course; arrested, probably–certainly detained. Examined, cross-examined, bully-ragged–I know something of the French police and their ways."

"If they stop us, I shall write to the *Times*" cried his brother, by profession a man of peace, but with a choleric eye that told of an angry temperament.

"By all means, my dear Silas, when you get the chance. That won't be just yet, for I tell you we're in a tight place, and may expect a good deal of worry." With that he took out his cigarette-case, and his match-box, lighted his cigarette, and calmly watched the smoke rising with all the coolness of an old campaigner accustomed to encounter and face the ups and downs of life. "I only hope to goodness they'll run straight on to Paris," he added in a fervent tone, not unmixed with apprehension. "No! By jingo, we're slackening speed–."

"Why shouldn't we? It's right the conductor, or chief of the train, or whatever you call him, should know what has happened."

"Why, man, can't you see? While the train is travelling express, everyone must stay on board it; if it slows, it is possible to leave it."

"Who would want to leave it?"

"Oh, I don't know," said the General, rather testily. "Any way, the thing's done now."

The train had pulled up in obedience to the signal of alarm given by someone in the sleeping-car, but by whom it was impossible to say. Not by the porter, for he seemed greatly surprised as the conductor came up to him.

"How did you know?" he asked.

"Know! Know what? You stopped me."

"I didn't."

"Who rang the bell, then?"

"I did not. But I'm glad you've come. There has been a crime–murder."

"Good Heavens!" cried the conductor, jumping up on to the car, and entering into the situation at once. His business was only to verify the fact, and take all necessary precautions. He was a burly, brusque, peremptory person, the despotic, self-important French official, who knew what to do–as he thought–and did it without hesitation or apology.

"No one must leave the car," he said in a tone not to be misunderstood. "Neither now, nor on arrival at the station."

There was a shout of protest and dismay, which he quickly cut short.

"You will have to arrange it with the authorities in Paris; they can alone decide. My duty is plain: to detain you, place you under surveillance till then. Afterwards, we will see. Enough, gentlemen and madame"–

He bowed with the instinctive gallantry of his nation to the female figure which now appeared at the door of her compartment. She stood for a moment listening, seemingly greatly agitated, and then, without a word, disappeared, retreating hastily into her own private room, where she shut herself in.

Almost immediately, at a signal from the conductor, the train resumed its journey. The distance remaining to be traversed was short; half an hour more, and the Lyons station, at Paris, was reached, where the bulk of the passengers–all, indeed, but the occupants of the sleeper–descended and passed through the barriers. The latter were again desired to keep their places, while a posse of officials came and mounted guard. Presently they were told to leave the car one by one, but to take nothing with them. All their hand-bags, rugs, and belongings were to remain in the berths, just as they lay. One by one they were marched under escort to a large and bare waiting-room, which had, no doubt, been prepared for their reception.

Here they took their seats on chairs placed at wide intervals apart, and were peremptorily forbidden to hold any communication with each other, by word or gesture. This order was enforced by a fierce-looking guard in blue and red uniform, who stood facing them with his arms folded, gnawing his moustache and frowning severely.

Last of all, the porter was brought in and treated like the passengers, but more distinctly as a prisoner. He had a guard all to himself; and it seemed as though he was the object of peculiar suspicion. It had no great effect upon him, for, while the rest of the party were very plainly sad, and a prey to lively apprehension, the porter sat dull and unmoved, with the stolid, sluggish, unconcerned aspect of a man just roused from sound sleep and relapsing into slumber, who takes little notice of what is passing around.

Meanwhile, the sleeping-car, with its contents, especially the corpse of the victim, was shunted into a siding, and sentries were placed on it at both ends. Seals had been affixed upon the entrance doors, so that the interior might be kept inviolate until it could be visited and examined by the Chef de la Sûreté, or Chief of the Detective Service. Everyone and everything awaited the arrival of this all-important functionary.

2

M. Floçon, the Chief, was an early man, and he paid a first visit to his office about 7 A.M.

He lived just round the corner in the Rue des Arcs, and had not far to go to the Prefecture. But even now, soon after daylight, he was correctly dressed, as became a responsible ministerial officer. He wore a tight frock coat and an immaculate white tie; under his arm he carried the regulation portfolio, or lawyer's bag, stuffed full of reports, dispositions, and documents dealing with cases in hand. He was altogether a very precise and natty little personage, quiet and unpretending in demeanour, with a mild, thoughtful face in which two small ferrety eyes blinked and twinkled behind gold-rimmed glasses. But when things went wrong, when he had to deal with fools, or when scent was keen, or the enemy near, he would become as fierce and eager as any terrier.

He had just taken his place at his table and begun to arrange his papers, which, being a man of method, he kept carefully sorted by lots each in an old copy of the *Figaro*, when he was called to the telephone. His services were greatly needed, as we know, at the Lyons station and the summons was to the following effect:

"Crime on train No. 45. A man murdered in the sleeper. All the passengers held. Please come at once. Most important."

A fiacre was called instantly, and M. Floçon, accompanied by Galipaud and Block, the two first inspectors for duty, was driven with all possible speed across Paris.

He was met outside the station, just under the wide verandah, by the officials, who gave him a brief outline of the facts, so far as they were known, and as they have already been put before the reader.

"The passengers have been detained?" asked M. Floçon at once.

"Those in the sleeping-car only—"

"Tut, tut! They should have been all kept—at least until you had taken their names and addresses. Who knows what they might not have been able to tell?"

It was suggested that as the crime was committed presumably while the train was in motion, only those in the one car could be implicated.

"We should never jump to conclusions," said the Chief snappishly. "Well, show me the train card—the list of the travellers in the sleeper."

"It cannot be found, sir."

"Impossible! Why, it is the porter's business to deliver it at the end of the journey to his superiors, and under the law—to us. Where is the porter? In custody?"

"Surely, sir, but there is something wrong with him."

"So I should think! Nothing of this kind could well occur without his knowledge. If he was doing his duty—unless, of course, he—but let us avoid hasty conjectures."

"He has also lost the passengers' tickets, which you know he retains till the end of the journey. After the catastrophe, however, he was unable to lay his hand upon his pocket-book. It contained all his papers."

"Worse and worse. There is something behind all this. Take me to him. Stay, can I have a private room close to the other—where the prisoners, those held on suspicion, are? It will be necessary to hold investigations, take their depositions. M. le Juge will be here directly."

M. Floçon was soon installed in a room actually communicating with the waiting-room, and as a preliminary of the first importance, taking precedence even of the examination of the sleeping-car, he ordered the porter to be brought in to answer certain questions.

The man, Ludwig Groote, as he presently gave his name, thirty-two years of age, born at Amsterdam, looked such a sluggish, slouching, blear-eyed creature that M. Floçon began by a sharp rebuke.

"Now. Sharp! Are you always like this?" cried the Chief. The porter still stared straight before him with lack-lustre eyes, and made no immediate reply.

"Are you drunk? are you—Can it be possible?" he said, and in vague reply to a sudden strong suspicion, he went on: "What were you doing between Laroche and Paris? Sleeping?"

The man roused himself a little. "I think I slept. I must have slept. I was very drowsy. I had been up two nights; but so it is always, and I am not like this generally. I do not understand."

"Hah!" The Chief thought he understood. "Did you feel this drowsiness before leaving Laroche?"

"No, monsieur, I did not. Certainly not. I was fresh till then—quite fresh."

"Hum; exactly; I see;" and the little Chief jumped to his feet and ran round to where the porter stood sheepishly, and sniffed and smelt at him.

"Yes, yes." Sniff, sniff, sniff, the little man danced round and round him, then took hold of the porter's head with one hand, and with the other turned down his lower eyelid so as to expose the eyeball, sniffed a little more, and then resumed his seat.

"Exactly. And now, where is your train card?"

"Pardon, monsieur, I cannot find it."

"That is absurd. Where do you keep it? Look again—search—I must have it."

The porter shook his head hopelessly.

"It is gone, monsieur, and my pocket-book."

"But your papers, the tickets—"

"Everything was in it, monsieur. I must have dropped it."

Strange, very strange. However—the fact was to be recorded, for the moment. He could of course return to it.

"You can give me the names of the passengers?"

"No, monsieur. Not exactly. I cannot remember, not enough to distinguish between them."

"*Fichtre*! But this is most devilishly irritating. To think that I have to do with a man so stupid–such an idiot, such an ass!"

"At least you know how the berths were occupied, how many in each, and which persons? Yes? You can tell me that? Well, go on. By and by we will have the passengers in, and you can fix their places, after I have ascertained their names. Now, please! For how many was the car?"

"Sixteen. There were two compartments of four berths each, and four of two berths each."

"Stay, let us make a plan. I will draw it. Here, now, is that right?" and the Chief held up the rough diagram.

"Here we have the six compartments. Now take *a*, with berths 1, 2, 3, and 4. Were they all occupied?"

"No; only two, by Englishmen. I know that they talked English, which I understand a little. One was a soldier; the other, I think, a clergyman, or priest."

"Good! we can verify that directly. Now, *b*, with berths 5 and 6. Who was there?"

"One gentleman. I don't remember his name. But I shall know him by appearance."

"Go on. In *c*, two berths, 7 and 8?"

"Also one gentleman. It was he who–I mean, that is where the crime occurred."

"Ah, indeed, in 7 and 8? Very well. And the next, 9 and 10?"

"A lady. Our only lady. She came from Rome."

"One moment. Where did the rest come from? Did any embark on the road?"

"No, monsieur; all the passengers travelled through from Rome."

"The dead man included? Was he Roman?"

"That I cannot say, but he came on board at Rome."

"Very well. This lady–she was alone?"

"In the compartment, yes. But not altogether."

"I do not understand!"

"She had her servant with her."

"In the car?"

"No, not in the car. As a passenger by second class. But she came to her mistress sometimes, in the car."

"For her service, I presume?"

"Well, yes, monsieur, when I would permit it. But she came a little too often, and I was compelled to protest, to speak to Madame la Comtesse—"

"She was a countess, then?"

"The maid addressed her by that title. That is all I know. I heard her."

"When did you see the lady's maid last?"

"Last night. I think at Amberieux. about 8 p.m."

"Not this morning?"

"No, sir, I am quite sure of that."

"Not at Laroche? She did not come on board to stay, for the last stage, when her mistress would be getting up, dressing, and likely to require her?"

"No; I should not have permitted it."

"And where is the maid now, d'you suppose?"

The porter looked at him with an air of complete imbecility.

"She is surely somewhere near, in or about the station. She would hardly desert her mistress now," he said, stupidly, at last.

"At any rate we can soon settle that." The Chief turned to one of his assistants, both of whom had been standing behind him all the time, and said:

"Step out, Galipaud, and see. No, wait. I am nearly as stupid as this simpleton. Describe this maid."

"Tall and slight, dark-eyed, very black hair. Dressed all in black, plain black bonnet. I cannot remember more."

"Find her, Galipaud—keep your eye on her. We may want her—why, I cannot say, as she seems disconnected with the event, but still she ought to be at hand." Then, turning to the porter, he went on. "Finish, please. You said 9 and 10 was the lady's. Well, 11 and 12?"

"It was vacant all through the run."

"And the last compartment, for four?"

"There were two berths, occupied both by Frenchmen, at least so I judged them. They talked French to each other and to me."

"Then now we have them all. Stand aside, please, and I will make the passengers come in. We will then determine their places and affix their names from their own admissions. Call them in, Block, one by one."

3

The questions put by M. Floçon were much the same in every case, and were limited in this early stage of the inquiry to the one point of identity.

The first who entered was a Frenchman. He was a jovial, fat-faced, portly man, who answered to the name of Anatole Lafolay, and who described himself as a traveller in precious stones. The berth he had occupied was No. 13 in compartment *f*. His companion in the berth was a younger man, smaller, slighter, but of much the same stamp. His name was Jules Devaux, and he was a commission agent. His berth had been No. 15 in the same compartment, f. Both these Frenchmen gave their addresses with the names of many people to whom they were well known, and established at once a reputation for respectability which was greatly in their favour.

The third to appear was the tall, gray-headed Englishman, who had taken a certain lead at the first discovery of the crime. He called himself General Sir Charles Collingham, an officer of her Majesty's army; and the clergyman who shared the compartment was his brother, the Reverend Silas Collingham, rector of Theakstone-Lammas, in the county of Norfolk. Their berths were numbered 1 and 4 in *a*.

Before the English General was dismissed, he asked whether he was likely to be detained.

"For the present, yes," replied M. Floçon, briefly. He did not care to be asked questions. That, under the circumstances, was his business.

"Because I should like to communicate with the British Embassy."

"You are known there?" asked the detective, not choosing to believe the story at first. It might be a ruse of some sort.

"I know Lord Dufferin personally; I was with him in India. Also Colonel Papillon, the military attaché; we were in the same regiment. If I sent to the Embassy, the latter would, no doubt, come himself."

"How do you propose to send?"

"That is for you to decide. All I wish is that it should be known that my brother and I are detained under suspicion, and incriminated."

"Hardly that, Monsieur le General. But it shall be as you wish. We will telephone from here to the post nearest the Embassy to inform his Excellency—"

"Certainly, Lord Dufferin, and my friend, Colonel Papillon."

"Of what has occurred. And now, if you will permit me to proceed?"

So the single occupant of the compartment *b*, that adjoining the Englishmen, was called in. He was an Italian, by name Natale Ripaldi; a dark-skinned man, with very black hair and a bristling black moustache. He wore a long dark cloak of the Inverness order, and, with the slouch hat he carried in his hand, and his downcast, secretive look, he had the rather conventional aspect of a conspirator.

"If monsieur permits," he volunteered to say after the formal questioning was over, "I can throw some light on this catastrophe."

"And how so, pray? Did you assist? Were you present? If so, why wait to speak till now?" said the detective, receiving the advance rather coldly. It behooved him to be very much on his guard.

"I have had no opportunity till now of addressing any one in authority. You are in authority, I presume?"

"I am the Chief of the Detective Service."

"Then, monsieur, remember, please, that I can give some useful information when called upon. Now, indeed, if you will receive it."

M. Floçon was so anxious to approach the inquiry without prejudice that he put up his hand.

"We will wait, if you please. When M. le Juge arrives, then, perhaps; at any rate, at a later stage. That will do now, thank you."

The Italian's lip curled with a slight indication of contempt at the French detective's methods, but he bowed without speaking, and went out.

Last of all the lady appeared, in a long sealskin travelling cloak, and closely veiled. She answered M. Floçon's questions in a low, tremulous voice, as though greatly perturbed.

She was the Contessa di Castagneto, she said, an Englishwoman by birth; but her husband had been an Italian, as the name implied, and they resided in Rome. He was dead–she had been a widow for two or three years, and was on her way now to London.

"That will do, madame, thank you," said the detective, politely, "for the present at least."

"Why, are we likely to be detained? I trust not." Her voice became appealing, almost piteous. Her hands, restlessly moving, showed how much she was distressed.

"Indeed, Madame la Comtesse, it must be so. I regret it infinitely; but until we have gone further into this, have elicited some facts, arrived at some conclusions–But there, madame, I need not, must not say more."

"Oh, monsieur, I was so anxious to continue my journey. Friends are awaiting me in London. I do hope–I most earnestly beg and entreat you to spare me. I am not very strong; my health is indifferent. Do, sir, be so good as to release me from–"

As she spoke, she raised her veil, and showed what no woman wishes to hide, least of all when seeking the good-will of one of the opposite sex. She had a handsome face–

strikingly so. Not even the long journey, the fatigue, the worries and anxieties which had supervened, could rob her of her marvellous beauty.

She was a brilliant brunette, dark-skinned; but her complexion was of a clear, pale olive, and as soft, as lustrous as pure ivory. Her great eyes, of a deep velvety brown, were saddened by near tears. She had rich red lips, the only colour in her face, and these, habitually slightly apart, showed pearly-white glistening teeth.

It was difficult to look at this charming woman without being affected by her beauty. M. Floçon was a Frenchman, gallant and impressionable; yet he steeled his heart. A detective must beware of sentiment, and he seemed to see something insidious in this appeal, which he resented.

"Madame, it is useless," he answered gruffly. "I do not make the law; I have only to support it. Every good citizen is bound to that."

"I trust I am a good citizen," said the Countess, with a wan smile, but very wearily. "Still, I should wish to be let off now. I have suffered greatly, terribly, by this horrible catastrophe. My nerves are quite shattered. It is too cruel. However, I can say no more, except to ask that you will let my maid come to me."

M. Floçon, still obdurate, would not even consent to that.

"I fear, madame, that for the present at least you cannot be allowed to communicate with any one, not even with your maid."

"But she is not implicated; she was not in the car. I have not seen her since—"

"Since?" repeated M. Floçon, after a pause.

"Since last night, at Amberieux, about eight o'clock. She helped me to undress, and saw me to bed. I sent her away then, and said I should not need her till we reached Paris. But I want her now, indeed I do."

"She did not come to you at Laroche?"

"No. Have I not said so? The porter,"–here she pointed to the man, who stood staring at her from the other side of the table,–"he made difficulties about her being in the car, saying that she came too often, stayed too long, that I must pay for her berth, and so on. I did not see why I should do that; so she stayed away."

"Except from time to time?"

"Precisely."

"And the last time was at Amberieux?"

"As I have told you, and he will tell you the same."

"Thank you, madame, that will do." The Chief rose from his chair, plainly intimating that the interview was at an end.

4

He had other work to do, and was eager to get at it. So he left Block to show the Countess back to the waiting-room, and, motioning to the porter that he might also go, the Chief hastened to the sleeping-car, the examination of which, too long delayed, claimed his urgent attention.

It is the first duty of a good detective to visit the actual theatre of a crime and overhaul it inch by inch,—seeking, searching, investigating, looking for any, even the most insignificant, traces of the murderer's hands.

The sleeping-car, as I have said, had been side-tracked, its doors were sealed, and it was under strict watch and ward. But everything, of course, gave way before the detective, and, breaking through the seals, he walked in, making straight for the little room or compartment where the body of the victim still lay untended and absolutely untouched.

It was a ghastly sight, although not new in M. Floçon's experience. There lay the corpse in the narrow berth, just as it had been stricken. It was partially undressed, wearing only shirt and drawers. The former lay open at the chest, and showed the gaping wound that had, no doubt, caused death, probably instantaneous death. But other blows had been struck; there must have been a struggle, fierce and embittered, as for dear life. The savage truculence of the murderer had triumphed, but not until he had battered in the face, destroying features and rendering recognition almost impossible.

A knife had given the mortal wound; that was at once apparent from the shape of the wound. It was the knife, too, which had gashed and stabbed the face, almost wantonly; for some of these wounds had not bled, and the plain inference was that they had been inflicted after life

had sped. M. Floçon examined the body closely, but
without disturbing it. The police medical officer would
wish to see it as it was found. The exact position, as well
as the nature of the wounds, might afford evidence as to
the manner of death.

But the Chief looked long, and with absorbed,
concentrated interest, at the murdered man, noting all he
actually saw, and conjecturing a good deal more.

The features of the mutilated face were all but
unrecognizable, but the hair, which was abundant, was
long, black, and inclined to curl; the black moustache was
thick and drooping. The shirt was of fine linen, the
drawers silk. On one finger were two good rings, the
hands were clean, the nails well kept, and there was
every evidence that the man did not live by manual
labour. He was of the easy, cultured class, as distinct
from the workman or operative.

This conclusion was borne out by his light baggage,
which still lay about the berth,—hat-box, rugs, umbrella,
brown morocco hand-bag. All were the property of
someone well to do, or at least possessed of decent
belongings. One or two pieces bore a monogram, "F.Q.,"
the same as on the shirt and under-linen; but on the bag
was a luggage label, with the name, "Francis Quadling,
passenger to Paris," in full. Its owner had apparently no
reason to conceal his name. More strangely, those who
had done him to death had been at no pains to remove all
traces of his identity.

M. Floçon opened the hand-bag, seeking for further
evidence; but found nothing of importance,—only loose
collars, cuffs, a sponge and slippers, two Italian
newspapers of an earlier date. No money, valuables, or
papers. All these had been removed probably, and
presumably, by the perpetrator of the crime.

Having settled the first preliminary but essential
points, he next surveyed the whole compartment
critically. Now, for the first time, he was struck with the
fact that the window was open to its full height.

Since when was this? It was a question to be put presently to the porter and any others who had entered the car, but the discovery drew him to examine the window more closely, and with good results.

At the ledge, caught on a projecting point on the far side, partly in, partly out of the car, was a morsel of white lace, a scrap of feminine apparel; although what part, or how it had come there, was not at once obvious to M. Floçon. A long and minute inspection of this bit of lace, which he was careful not to detach as yet from the place in which he found it, showed that it was ragged, and frayed, and fast caught where it hung. It could not have been blown there by any chance air; it must have been torn from the article to which it belonged, whatever that might be,—head-dress, nightcap, night-dress, or handkerchief. The lace was of a kind to serve any of these purposes.

Inspecting further, M. Floçon made a second discovery. On the small table under the window was a short length of black jet beading, part of the trimming or ornamentation of a lady's dress.

These two objects of feminine origin—one partly outside the car, the other near it, but quite inside—gave rise to many conjectures. It led, however, to the inevitable conclusion that a woman had been at some time or other in the berth. M. Floçon could not but connect these two finds with the fact of the open window. The latter might, of course, have been the work of the murdered man himself at an earlier hour. Yet it is unusual, as the detective imagined, for a passenger, and especially an Italian, to lie under an open window in a sleeping-berth when travelling by express train before daylight in March.

Who opened that window, then, and why? Perhaps some further facts might be found on the outside of the car. With this idea, M. Floçon left it, and passed on to the line or permanent way.

Here he found himself a good deal below the level of the car. These sleepers have no foot-boards like ordinary carriages; access to them is gained from a platform by the steps at each end. The Chief was short of stature, and he could only approach the window outside by calling one of the guards and ordering him to make the small ladder (*faire la petite echelle*). This meant stooping and giving a back, on which little M. Floçon climbed nimbly, and so was raised to the necessary height.

A close scrutiny revealed nothing unusual. The exterior of the car was encrusted with the mud and dust gathered in the journey, none of which appeared to have been disturbed.

M. Floçon reentered the carriage neither disappointed nor pleased; his mind was in an open state, ready to receive any impressions, and as yet only one that was at all clear and distinct was borne in on him.

This was the presence of the lace and the jet beads in the theatre of the crime. The inference was fair and simple. He came logically and surely to this:

1. That some woman had entered the compartment.

2. That whether or not she had come in before the crime, she was there after the window had been opened, which was not done by the murdered man.

3. That she had leaned out, or partly passed out, of the window at some time or other, as the scrap of lace testified.

4. Why had she leaned out? To seek some means of exit or escape, of course.

But escape from whom? From what? The murderer? Then she must know him, and unless an accomplice (if so, why run from him?), she would give up her knowledge on compulsion, if not voluntarily, as seemed doubtful, seeing she (his suspicions were consolidating) had not done so already.

But there might be another even stronger reason to attempt escape at such imminent risk as leaving an express train at full speed. To escape from her own act and the consequences it must entail–escape from horror first, from detection next, and then from arrest and punishment.

All this would imperiously impel even a weak woman to face the worst peril, to look out, lean out, even try the terrible but impossible feat of climbing out of the car.

So M. Floçon, by fair process of reasoning, reached a point which incriminated one woman, the only woman possible, and that was the titled, high-bred lady who called herself the Contessa di Castagneto.

This conclusion gave a definite direction to further search. Consulting the rough plan which he had constructed to take the place of the missing train card, he entered the compartment which the Countess had occupied, and which was actually next door.

It was in the tumbled, untidy condition of a sleeping-place but just vacated. The sex and quality of its recent occupant were plainly apparent in the goods and chattels lying about, the property and possessions of a delicate, well-bred woman of the world, things still left as she had used them last–rugs still unrolled, a pair of easy-slippers on the floor, the sponge in its waterproof bag on the bed, brushes, bottles, button-hook, hand-glass, many things belonging to the dressing-bag, not yet returned to that receptacle. The maid was no doubt to have attended to all these, but as she had not come, they remained unpacked and strewn about in some disorder.

M. Floçon pounced down upon the contents of the berth, and commenced an immediate search for a lace scarf, or any wrap or cover with lace.

He found nothing, and was hardly disappointed. It told more against the Countess, who, if innocent, would have no reason to conceal or make away with a possibly incriminating possession, the need for which she could not of course understand.

Next, he handled the dressing-bag, and with deft fingers replaced everything.

Everything was forthcoming but one glass bottle, a small one, the absence of which he noted, but thought of little consequence, till, by and by, he came upon it under peculiar circumstances.

Before leaving the car, and after walking through the other compartments, M. Floçon made an especially strict search of the corner where the porter had his own small chair, his only resting-place, indeed, throughout the journey. He had not forgotten the attendant's condition when first examined, and he had even then been nearly satisfied that the man had been hocussed, narcotized, drugged.

Any doubts were entirely removed by his picking up near the porter's seat a small silver-topped bottle and a handkerchief, both marked with coronet and monogram, the last of which, although the letters were much interlaced and involved, were decipherable as S.L.L.C.

It was that of the Countess, and corresponded with the marks on her other belongings. He put it to his nostril, and recognized at once by its smell that it had contained tincture of laudanum, or some preparation of that drug.

5

M. Floçon was an experienced detective, and he knew so well that he ought to be on his guard against the most plausible suggestions, that he did not like to make too much of these discoveries. Still, he was distinctly satisfied, if not exactly exultant, and he went back towards the station with a strong predisposition against the Contessa di Castagneto.

Just outside the waiting-room, however, his assistant, Galipaud, met him with news which rather dashed his hopes, and gave a new direction to his thoughts.

The lady's maid was not to be found.

"Impossible!" cried the Chief, and then at once suspicion followed surprise.

"I have looked, monsieur, inquired everywhere; the maid has not been seen. She certainly is not here."

"Did she go through the barrier with the other passengers?"

"No one knows; no one remembers her; not even the conductor. But she has gone. That is positive."

"Yet it was her duty to be here; to attend to her service. Her mistress would certainly want her–has asked for her! Why should she run away?"

This question presented itself as one of infinite importance, to be pondered over seriously before he went further into the inquiry.

Did the Countess know of this disappearance?

She had asked imploringly for her maid. True, but might that not be a blind? Women are born actresses, and at need can assume any part, convey any impression. Might not the Countess have wished to be dissociated from the maid, and therefore have affected complete ignorance of her flight?

"I will try her further," said M. Floçon to himself.

But then, supposing that the maid had taken herself off of her own accord? Why was it? Why had she done so? Because—because she was afraid of something. If so, of what? No direct accusation could be brought against her on the face of it. She had not been in the sleeping-car at the time of the murder, while the Countess as certainly was; and, according to strong presumption, in the very compartment where the deed was done. If the maid was afraid, why was she afraid?

Only on one possible hypothesis. That she was either in collusion with the Countess, or possessed of some guilty knowledge tending to incriminate the Countess and probably herself. She had run away to avoid any inconvenient questioning tending to get her mistress into trouble, which would react probably on herself.

"We must press the Countess on this point closely; I will put it plainly to M. le Juge," said the detective, as he entered the private room set apart for the police authorities, where he found M. Beaumont le Hardi, the instructing judge, and the Commissary of the Quartier (arrondissement).

A lengthy conference followed among the officials. M. Floçon told all he knew, all he had discovered, gave his views with all the force and fluency of a public prosecutor, and was congratulated warmly on the progress he had made.

"I agree with you, sir," said the instructing judge: "we must have in the Countess first, and pursue the line indicated as regards the missing maid."

"I will fetch her, then. Stay, what can be going on in there?" cried M. Floçon, rising from his seat and running into the outer waiting-room, which, to his surprise and indignation, he found in great confusion.

The guard who was on duty was struggling, in personal conflict almost, with the English General. There was a great hubbub of voices, and the Countess was lying back half-fainting in her chair.

"What's all this? How dare you, sir?"

This to the General, who now had the man by the throat with one hand and with the other was preventing him from drawing his sword. "Desist–forbear! You are opposing legal authority; desist, or I will call in assistance and will have you secured and removed."

The little Chief's blood was up; he spoke warmly, with all the force and dignity of an official who sees the law outraged.

"It is entirely the fault of this ruffian of yours; he has behaved most brutally," replied Sir Charles, still holding him tight.

"Let him go, monsieur; your behaviour is inexcusable. What! you, a military officer of the highest rank, to assault a sentinel! For shame! This is unworthy of you!"

"He deserves to be scragged, the beast!" went on the General, as with one sharp turn of the wrist he threw the guard off, and sent him flying nearly across the room, where, being free at last, the Frenchman drew his sword and brandished it threateningly–from a distance.

But M. Floçon interposed with uplifted hand and insisted upon an explanation.

"It is just this," replied Sir Charles, speaking fast and with much fierceness: "that lady there–poor thing, she is ill, you can see that for yourself, suffering, overwrought; she asked for a glass of water, and this brute, triple brute, as you say in French, refused to bring it."

"I could not leave the room," protested the guard. "My orders were precise."

"So I was going to fetch the water," went on the General angrily, eying the guard as though he would like to make another grab at him, "and this fellow interfered."

"Very properly," added M. Floçon.

"Then why didn't he go himself, or call someone? Upon my word, monsieur, you are not to be complimented upon your people, nor your methods. I used to think that a Frenchman was gallant, courteous, especially to ladies."

The Chief looked a little disconcerted, but remembering what he knew against this particular lady, he stiffened and said severely, "I am responsible for my conduct to my superiors, and not to you. Besides, you appear to forget your position. You are here, detained–all of you"–he spoke to the whole room–"under suspicion. A ghastly crime has been perpetrated–by someone among you–"

"Do not be too sure of that," interposed the irrepressible General.

"Who else could be concerned? The train never stopped after leaving Laroche," said the detective, allowing himself to be betrayed into argument.

"Yes, it did," corrected Sir Charles, with a contemptuous laugh; "shows how much you know."

Again the Chief looked unhappy. He was on dangerous ground, face to face with a new fact affecting all his theories,–if fact it was, not mere assertion, and that he must speedily verify. But nothing was to be gained–much, indeed, might be lost–by prolonging this discussion in the presence of the whole party. It was entirely opposed to the French practice of investigation, which works secretly, taking witnesses separately, one by one, and strictly preventing all intercommunication or collusion among them.

"What I know or do not know is my affair," he said, with an indifference he did not feel. "I shall call upon you, M. le Général, for your statement in due course, and that of the others." He bowed stiffly to the whole room. "Everyone must be interrogated. M. le Juge is now here, and he proposes to begin, madame, with you."

The Countess gave a little start, shivered, and turned very pale.

"Can't you see she is not equal to it?" cried the General, hotly. "She has not yet recovered. In the name of–I do not say chivalry, for that would be useless–but of common humanity, spare madame, at least for the present."

"That is impossible, quite impossible. There are reasons why Madame la Comtesse should be examined first. I trust, therefore, she will make an effort."

"I will try, if you wish it." She rose from her chair and walked a few steps rather feebly, then stopped.

"No, no, Countess, do not go," said Sir Charles, hastily, in English, as he moved across to where she stood and gave her his hand. "This is sheer cruelty, sir, and cannot be permitted."

"Stand aside!" shouted M. Floçon; "I forbid you to approach that lady, to address her, or communicate with her. Guard, advance, do your duty."

But the guard, although his sword was still out of its sheath, showed great reluctance to move. He had no desire to try conclusions again with this very masterful person, who was, moreover, a general; as he had seen service, he had a deep respect for generals, even of foreign growth.

Meanwhile the General held his ground and continued his conversation with the Countess, speaking still in English, thus exasperating M. Floçon, who did not understand the language, almost to madness.

"This is not to be borne!" he cried. "Here, Galipaud, Block;" and when his two trusty assistants came rushing in, he pointed furiously to the General. "Seize him, remove him by force if necessary. He shall go to the *violon*–to the nearest lock-up."

The noise attracted also the Judge and the Commissary, and there were now six officials in all, including the guard, all surrounding the General, a sufficiently imposing force to overawe even the most recalcitrant fire-eater.

But now the General seemed to see only the comic side of the situation, and he burst out laughing.

"What, all of you? How many more? Why not bring up cavalry and artillery, horse, foot, and guns?" he asked, derisively. "All to prevent one old man from offering his services to one weak woman! Gentlemen, my regards!"

"Really, Charles, I fear you are going too far," said his brother the clergyman, who, however, had been manifestly enjoying the whole scene.

"Indeed, yes. It is not necessary, I assure you," added the Countess, with tears of gratitude in her big brown eyes. "I am most touched, most thankful. You are a true soldier, a true English gentleman, and I shall never forget your kindness." Then she put her hand in his with a pretty, winning gesture that was reward enough for any man.

Meanwhile, the Judge, the senior official present, had learned exactly what had happened, and he now addressed the General with a calm but stern rebuke.

"Monsieur will not, I trust, oblige us to put in force the full power of the law. I might, if I chose, and as I am fully entitled, commit you at once to Mazas, to keep you in solitary confinement. Your conduct has been deplorable, well calculated to traverse and impede justice. But I am willing to believe that you were led away, not unnaturally, as a gallant gentleman,—it is the characteristic of your nation, of your cloth,—and that on more mature consideration you will acknowledge and not repeat your error."

M. Beaumont le Hardi was a grave, florid, soft-voiced person, with a bald head and a comfortably-lined white waistcoat; one who sought his ends by persuasion, not force, but who had the instincts of a gentleman, and little sympathy with the peremptory methods of his more inflammable colleague.

"Oh, with all my heart, monsieur," said Sir Charles, cordially. "You saw, or at least know, how this has occurred. I did not begin it, nor was I the most to blame. But I was in the wrong, I admit. What do you wish me to do now?"

"Give me your promise to abide by our rules,–they may be irksome, but we think them necessary,–and hold no further converse with your companions."

"Certainly, certainly, monsieur,–at least after I have said one word more to Madame la Comtesse."

"No, no, I cannot permit even that–"

But Sir Charles, in spite of the warning finger held up by the Judge, insisted upon crying out to her, as she was being led into the other room:

"Courage, dear lady, courage. Don't let them bully you. You have nothing to fear."

Any further defiance of authority was now prevented by her almost forcible removal from the room.

6

The stormy episode just ended had rather a disturbing effect on M. Floçon, who could scarcely give his full attention to all the points, old and new, that had now arisen in the investigation. But he would have time to go over them at his leisure, while the work of interrogation was undertaken by the Judge.

The latter had taken his seat at a small table, and just opposite was his *greffier*, or clerk, who was to write down question and answer, *verbatim*. A little to one side, with the light full on the face, the witness was seated, bearing the scrutiny of three pairs of eyes–the Judge first, and behind him, those of the Chief Detective and the Commissary of Police.

"I trust, madame, that you are equal to answering a few questions?" began M. le Hardi, blandly.

"Oh, yes, I hope so. Indeed, I have no choice," replied the Countess, bravely resigned.

"They will refer principally to your maid."

"Ah!" said the Countess, quickly and in a troubled voice, yet she bore the gaze of the three officials without flinching.

"I want to know a little more about her, if you please."

"Of course. Anything I know I will tell you." She spoke now with perfect self-possession. "But if I might ask–why this interest?"

"I will tell you frankly. You asked for her, we sent for her, and–"

"Yes?"

"She cannot be found. She is not in the station."

The Countess all but jumped from her chair in her surprise–surprise that seemed too spontaneous to be feigned.

"Impossible! it cannot be. She would not dare to leave me here like this, all alone."

"*Parbleu!* she has dared. Most certainly she is not here."

"But what can have become of her?"

"Ah, madame, what indeed? Can you form any idea? We hoped you might have been able to enlighten us."

"I cannot, monsieur, not in the least."

"Perchance you sent her on to your hotel to warn your friends that you were detained? To fetch them, perhaps, to you in your trouble?"

The trap was neatly contrived, but she was not deceived.

"How could I? I knew of no trouble when I saw her last."

"Oh, indeed? And when was that?"

"Last night, at Amberieux, as I have already told that gentleman." She pointed to M. Floçon, who was obliged to nod his head.

"Well, she has gone away somewhere. It does not much matter, still it is odd, and for your sake we should like to help you to find her, if you do wish to find her?"

Another little trap which failed.

"Indeed I hardly think she is worth keeping after this barefaced desertion."

"No, indeed. And she must be held to strict account for it, must justify it, give her reasons. So we must find her for you–"

"I am not at all anxious, really," the Countess said, quickly, and the remark told against her.

"Well, now, Madame la Comtesse, as to her description. Will you tell us what was her height, figure, colour of eyes, hair, general appearance?"

"She was tall, above the middle height, at least; slight, good figure, black hair and eyes."

"Pretty?"

"That depends upon what you mean by 'pretty.' Some people might think so, in her own class."

"How was she dressed?"

"In plain dark serge, bonnet of black straw and brown ribbons. I do not allow my maid to wear colours."

"Exactly. And her name, age, place of birth?"

"Hortense Petitpré, thirty-two, born, I believe, in Paris."

The Judge, when these particulars had been given, looked over his shoulder towards the detective, but said nothing. It was quite unnecessary, for M. Floçon, who had been writing in his note-book, now rose and left the room. He called Galipaud to him, saying sharply:

"Here is the more detailed description of the lady's maid, and in writing. Have it copied and circulate it at once. Give it to the station-master, and to the agents of police round about here. I have an idea—only an idea—that this woman has not gone far. It may be worth nothing, still there is the chance. People who are wanted often hang about the very place they would *not* stay in if they were wise. Anyhow, set a watch for her and come back here."

Meanwhile, the Judge had continued his questioning.

"And where, madame, did you obtain your maid?"

"In Rome. She was there, out of a place. I heard of her at an agency and registry office, when I was looking for a maid a month or two ago."

"Then she has not been long in your service?"

"No; as I tell you, she came to me in December last."

"Well recommended?"

"Strongly. She had lived with good families, French and English."

"And with you, what was her character?"

"Irreproachable."

"Well, so much for Hortense Petitpré. She is not far off, I dare say. When we want her we shall be able to lay hands on her, I do not doubt, madame may rest assured."

"Pray take no trouble in the matter. I certainly should not keep her."

"Very well, very well. And now, another small matter. I see," he referred to the rough plan of the sleeping-car prepared by M. Floçon,–"I see that you occupied the compartment *d*, with berths Nos. 9 and 10?"

"I think 9 was the number of my berth."

"It was. You may be certain of that. Now next door to your compartment–do you know who was next door? I mean in 7 and 8?"

The Countess's lip quivered, and she was a prey to sudden emotion as she answered in a low voice:

"It was where–where–"

"There, there, madame," said the Judge, reassuring her as he would a little child. "You need not say. It is no doubt very distressing to you. Yet, you know?"

She bent her head slowly, but uttered no word.

"Now this man, this poor man, had you noticed him at all? No–no–not afterwards, of course. It would not be likely. But during the journey. Did you speak to him, or he to you?"

"No, no–distinctly no."

"Nor see him?"

"Yes, I saw him, I believe, at Modane with the rest when we dined."

"Ah! exactly so. He dined at Modane. Was that the only occasion on which you saw him? You had never met him previously in Rome, where you resided?"

"Whom do you mean? The murdered man?"

"Who else?"

"No, not that I am aware of. At least I did not recognize him as a friend."

"I presume, if he was among your friends–"

"Pardon me, that he certainly was not," interrupted the Countess.

"Well, among your acquaintances–he would probably have made himself known to you?"

"I suppose so."

"And he did not do so? He never spoke to you, nor you to him?"

"I never saw him, the occupant of that compartment, except on that one occasion. I kept a good deal in my compartment during the journey."

"Alone? It must have been very dull for you," said the Judge, pleasantly.

"I was not always alone," said the Countess, hesitatingly, and with a slight flush. "I had friends in the car."

"Oh–oh"–the exclamation was long-drawn and rather significant.

"Who were they? You may as well tell us, madame, we should certainly find out."

"I have no wish to withhold the information," she replied, now turning pale, possibly at the imputation conveyed. "Why should I?"

"And these friends were–?"

"Sir Charles Collingham and his brother. They came and sat with me occasionally; sometimes one, sometimes the other."

"During the day?"

"Of course, during the day." Her eyes flashed, as though the question was another offence.

"Have you known them long?"

"The General I met in Roman society last winter. It was he who introduced his brother."

"Very good, so far. The General knew you, took an interest in you. That explains his strange, unjustifiable conduct just now–"

"I do not think it was either strange or unjustifiable," interrupted the Countess, hotly. "*He* is a gentleman."

"Quite a *preux cavalier*, of course. But we will pass on. You are not a good sleeper, I believe, madame?"

"Indeed no, I sleep badly, as a rule."

"Then you would be easily disturbed. Now, last night, did you hear anything strange in the car, more particularly in the adjoining compartment?"

"Nothing."

"No sound of voices raised high, no noise of a conflict, a struggle?"

"No, monsieur."

"That is odd. I cannot understand it. We know, beyond all question, from the appearance of the body,–the corpse,–that there was a fight, an encounter. Yet you, a wretched sleeper, with only a thin plank of wood between you and the affray, hear nothing, absolutely nothing. It is *most* extraordinary."

"I was asleep. I must have been asleep."

"A light sleeper would certainly be awakened. How can you explain–how can you reconcile that?" The question was blandly put, but the Judge's incredulity verged upon actual insolence.

"Easily: I had taken a soporific. I always do, on a journey. I am obliged to keep something, sulphonal or chloral, by me, on purpose."

"Then this, madame, is yours?" And the Judge, with an air of undisguised triumph, produced the small glass vial which M. Floçon had picked up in the sleeping-car near the conductor's seat.

The Countess, with a quick gesture, put out her hand to take it.

"No, I cannot give it up. Look as near as you like, and say is it yours?"

"Of course it is mine. Where did you get it? Not in my berth?"

"No, madame, not in your berth."

"But where?"

"Pardon me, we shall not tell you–not just now."

"I missed it last night," went on the Countess, slightly confused.

"After you had taken your dose of chloral?"

"No, before."

"And why did you want this? It is laudanum."

"For my nerves. I have a toothache. I–I–really, sir, I need not tell you all my ailments."

"And the maid had removed it?"

"So I presume; she must have taken it out of the bag in the first instance."

"And then kept it?"

"That is what I can only suppose."

"Ah!"

7

When the Judge had brought down the interrogation of the Countess to the production of the small glass bottle, he paused, and with a long-drawn "Ah!" of satisfaction, looked round at his colleagues.

Both M. Floçon and the Commissary nodded their heads approvingly, plainly sharing his triumph.

Then they all put their heads together in close, whispered conference.

"Admirable, M. le Juge!" said the detective. "You have been most adroit. It is a clear case."

"No doubt," said the Commissary, who was a blunt, rather coarse person, believing that to take anybody and everybody into custody is always the safest and simplest course. "It looks black against her. I think she ought to be arrested at once."

"We might, indeed we ought to have more evidence, more definite evidence, perhaps?" The Judge was musing over the facts as he knew them. "I should like, before going further, to look at the car," he said, suddenly coming to a conclusion.

M. Floçon readily agreed. "We will go together," he said, adding, "Madame will remain here, please, until we return. It may not be for long."

"And afterwards?" asked the Countess, whose nervousness had if anything increased during the whispered colloquy of the officials.

"Ah, afterwards! Who knows?" was the reply, with a shrug of the shoulders, all most enigmatic and unsatisfactory.

"What have we against her?" said the Judge, as soon as they had gained the absolute privacy of the sleeping-car.

"The bottle of laudanum and the porter's condition. He was undoubtedly drugged," answered the detective; and the discussion which followed took the form of a dialogue between them, for the Commissary took no part in it.

"Yes; but why by the Countess? How do we know that positively?"

"It is her bottle," said M. Floçon.

"Her story may be true–that she missed it, that the maid took it."

"We have nothing whatever against the maid. We know nothing about her."

"No. Except that she has disappeared. But that tells more against her mistress. It is all very vague. I do not see my way quite, as yet."

"But the fragment of lace, the broken beading? Surely, M. le Juge, they are a woman's, and only one woman was in the car–"

"So far as we know."

"But if these could be proved to be hers?"

"Ah! if you could prove that!"

"Easy enough. Have her searched, here at once, in the station. There is a female searcher attached to the detention-room."

"It is a strong measure. She is a lady."

"Ladies who commit crimes must not expect to be handled with kid gloves."

"She is an Englishwoman, or with English connections; titled, too. I hesitate, upon my word. Suppose we are wrong? It may lead to unpleasantness. M. le Prefet is anxious to avoid complications possibly international."

As he spoke, he bent over, and, taking a magnifier from his pocket, examined the lace, which still fluttered where it was caught.

"It is fine lace, I think. What say you, M. Floçon? You may be more experienced in such matters."

"The finest, or nearly so; I believe it is Valenciennes–the trimming of some underclothing, I should think. That surely is sufficient, M. le Juge?"

M. Beaumont le Hardi gave a reluctant consent, and the Chief went back himself to see that the searching was undertaken without loss of time.

The Countess protested, but vainly, against this new indignity. What could she do? A prisoner, practically friendless,–for the General was not within reach,–to resist was out of the question. Indeed, she was plainly told that force would be employed unless she submitted with a good grace. There was nothing for it but to obey.

Mother Tontaine, as the female searcher called herself, was an evil-visaged, corpulent old creature, with a sickly, soft, insinuating voice, and a greasy, familiar manner that was most offensive. They had given her the scrap of torn lace and the débris of the jet as a guide, with very particular directions to see if they corresponded with any part of the lady's apparel.

She soon showed her quality.

"Aha! oho! What is this, my pretty princess? How comes so great a lady into the hands of Mother Tontaine? But I will not harm you, my beauty, my pretty, my little one. Oh, no, no, I will not trouble you, dearie. No, trust to me;" and she held out one skinny claw, and looked the other way. The Countess did not or would not understand. "Madame has money?" went on the old hag in a half-threatening, half-coaxing whisper, as she came up quite close, and fastened on her victim like a bird of prey.

"If you mean that I am to bribe you–"

"Fie, the nasty word! But just a small present, a pretty gift, one or two yellow bits, twenty, thirty, forty francs–you'd better." She shook the soft arm she held roughly, and anything seemed preferable than to be touched by this horrible woman.

"Wait, wait!" cried the Countess, shivering all over, and, feeling hastily for her purse, she took out several napoleons.

"Aha! oho! One, two, three," said the searcher in a fat, wheedling voice. "Four, yes, four, five;" and she clinked the coins together in her palm, while a covetous light came into her faded eyes at the joyous sound. "Five—make it five at once, d'ye hear me?—or I'll call them in and tell them. That will go against you, my princess. What, try to bribe a poor old woman, Mother Tontaine, honest and incorruptible Tontaine? Five, then, five!"

With trembling haste the Countess emptied the whole contents of her purse in the old hag's hand.

"*Bon aubaine.* Nice pickings. It is a misery what they pay me here. I am, oh, so poor, and I have children, many babies. You will not tell them—the police—you dare not. No, no, no."

Thus muttering to herself, she shambled across the room to a corner, where she stowed the money safely away. Then she came back, showed the bit of lace, and pressed it into the Countess's hands.

"Do you know this, little one? Where it comes from, where there is much more? I was told to look for it, to search for it on you;" and with a quick gesture she lifted the edge of the Countess's skirt, dropping it next moment with a low, chuckling laugh.

"Oho! aha! You were right, my pretty, to pay me, my pretty—right. And some day, to-day, to-morrow, whenever I ask you, you will remember Mother Tontaine."

The Countess listened with dismay. What had she done? Put herself into the power of this greedy and unscrupulous old beldame?

"And this, my princess? What have we here, aha?"

Mère Tontaine held up next the broken bit of jet ornament for inspection, and as the Countess leaned forward to examine it more closely, gave it into her hand.

"You recognize it, of course. But be careful, my pretty! Beware! If anyone were looking, it would ruin you. I could not save you then. Sh! say nothing, only look, and quick, give it me back. I must have it to show."

All this time the Countess was turning the jet over and over in her open palm, with a perplexed, disturbed, but hardly a terrified air.

Yes, she knew it, or thought she knew it. It had been– But how had it come here, into the possession of this base myrmidon of the French police?

"Give it me, quick!" There was a loud knock at the door. "They are coming. Remember!" Mother Tontaine put her long finger to her lip. "Not a word! I have found nothing, of course. Nothing, I can swear to that, and you will not forget Mother Tontaine?"

Now M. Floçon stood at the open door awaiting the searcher's report. He looked much disconcerted when the old woman took him on one side and briefly explained that the search had been altogether fruitless.

There was nothing to justify suspicion, nothing, so far as she could find.

The detective looked from one to the other–from the hag he had employed in this unpleasant quest, to the lady on whom it had been tried. The Countess, to his surprise, did not complain. He had expected further and strong upbraidings. Strange to say, she took it very quietly. There was no indignation in her face. She was still pale, and her hands trembled, but she said nothing, made no reference, at least, to what she had just gone through.

Again he took counsel with his colleague, while the Countess was kept apart.

"What next, M. Floçon?" asked the Judge. "What shall we do with her?"

"Let her go," answered the detective, briefly.

"What! do you suggest this, sir," said the Judge, slyly. "After your strong and well-grounded suspicions?"

"They are as strong as ever, stronger: and I feel sure I shall yet justify them. But what I wish now is to let her go at large, under surveillance."

"Ah! you would shadow her?"

"Precisely. By a good agent. Galipaud, for instance. He speaks English, and he can, if necessary, follow her anywhere, even to England."

"She can be extradited," said the Commissary, with his one prominent idea of arrest.

"Do you agree, M. le Juge? Then, if you will permit me, I will give the necessary orders, and perhaps you will inform the lady that she is free to leave the station?"

The Countess now had reason to change her opinion of the French officials. Great politeness now replaced the first severity that had been so cruel. She was told, with many bows and apologies, that her regretted but unavoidable detention was at an end. Not only was she freely allowed to depart, but she was escorted by both M. Floçon and the Commissary outside, to where an omnibus was in waiting, and all her baggage piled on top, even to the dressing-bag, which had been neatly repacked for her.

But the little silver-topped vial had not been restored to her, nor the handkerchief.

In her joy at her deliverance, either she had not given these a second thought, or she did not wish to appear anxious to recover them.

Nor did she notice that, as the bus passed through the gates at the bottom of the large slope that leads from the Lyons Station, it was followed at a discreet distance by a modest fiacre, which pulled up, eventually, outside the Hôtel Madagascar. Its occupant, M. Galipaud, kept the Countess in sight, and, entering the hotel at her heels, waited till she had left the office, when he held a long conference with the proprietor.

8

A first stage in the inquiry had now been reached, with results that seemed promising, and were yet contradictory.

No doubt the watch to be set on the Countess might lead to something yet–something to bring first plausible suspicion to a triumphant issue; but the examination of the other occupants of the car should not be allowed to slacken on that account. The Countess might have some confederate among them–this pestilent English General, perhaps, who had made himself so conspicuous in her defence; or someone of them might throw light upon her movements, upon her conduct during the journey.

Then, with a spasm of self-reproach, M. Floçon remembered that two distinct suggestions had been made to him by two of the travellers, and that, so far, he had neglected them. One was the significant hint from the Italian that he could materially help the inquiry. The other was the General's sneering assertion that the train had not continued its journey uninterruptedly between Laroche and Paris.

Consulting the Judge, and laying these facts before him, it was agreed that the Italian's offer seemed the most important, and he was accordingly called in next.

"Who and what are you?" asked the Judge, carelessly, but the answer roused him at once to intense interest, and he could not quite resist a glance of reproach at M. Floçon.

"My name I have given you–Natale Ripaldi. I am a detective officer belonging to the Roman police."

"What!" cried M. Floçon, colouring deeply. "This is unheard of. Why in the name of all the devils have you withheld this most astonishing statement until now?"

"Monsieur surely remembers. I told him half an hour ago I had something important to communicate—"

"Yes, yes, of course. But why were you so reticent. Good Heavens!"

"Monsieur was not so encouraging that I felt disposed to force on him what I knew he would have to hear in due course."

"It is monstrous—quite abominable, and shall not end here. Your superiors shall hear of your conduct," went on the Chief, hotly.

"They will also hear, and, I think, listen to my version of the story,—that I offered you fairly, and at the first opportunity, all the information I had, and that you refused to accept it."

"You should have persisted. It was your manifest duty. You are an officer of the law, or you say you are."

"Pray telegraph at once, if you think fit, to Rome, to the police authorities, and you will find that Natale Ripaldi—your humble servant—travelled by the through express with their knowledge and authority. And here are my credentials, my official card, some official letters—"

"And what, in a word, have you to tell us?"

"I can tell you who the murdered man was."

"We know that already."

"Possibly; but only his name, I apprehend. I know his profession, his business, his object in travelling, for I was appointed to watch and follow him. That is why I am here."

"Was he a suspicious character, then? A criminal?"

"At any rate he was absconding from Rome, with valuables."

"A thief, in fact?"

The Italian put out the palms of his hands with a gesture of doubt and deprecation.

"Thief is a hard, ugly word. That which he was removing was, or had been, his own property."

"Tut, tut! do be more explicit and get on," interrupted the little Chief, testily.

"I ask nothing better; but if questions are put to me—"
The Judge interposed.

"Give us your story. We can interrogate you afterwards."

"The murdered man is Francis A. Quadling, of the firm of Correse & Quadling, bankers, in the Via Condotti, Rome. It was an old house, once of good, of the highest repute, but of late years it has fallen into difficulties. Its financial soundness was doubted in certain circles, and the Government was warned that a great scandal was imminent. So the matter was handed over to the police, and I was directed to make inquiries, and to keep my eye on this Quadling"—he jerked his thumb towards the platform, where the body might be supposed to be.

"This Quadling was the only surviving partner. He was well known and liked in Rome, indeed, many who heard the adverse reports disbelieved them, I myself among the number. But my duty was plain—"

"Naturally," echoed the fiery little detective.

"I made it my business to place the banker under surveillance, to learn his habits, his ways of life, see who were his friends, the houses he visited. I soon knew much that I wanted to know, although not all. But one fact I discovered, and think it right to inform you of it at once. He was on intimate terms with La Castagneto—at least, he frequently called upon her."

"La Castagneto! Do you mean the Countess of that name, who was a passenger in the sleeper?"

"Beyond doubt! it is she I mean." The officials looked at each other eagerly, and M. Beaumont le Hardi quickly turned over the sheets on which the Countess's evidence was recorded.

She had denied acquaintance with this murdered man, Quadling, and here was positive evidence that they were on intimate terms!

"He was at her house on the very day we all left Rome—in the evening, towards dusk. The Countess had

an apartment in the Via Margutta, and when he left her
he returned to his own place in the Condotti, entered the
bank, stayed half an hour, then came out with one hand-
bag and rug, called a cab, and was driven straight to the
railway station."

"And you followed?"

"Of course. When I saw him walk straight to the
sleeping-car, and ask the conductor for 7 and 8, I knew
that his plans had been laid, and that he was on the point
of leaving Rome secretly. When, presently, La Castagneto
also arrived, I concluded that she was in his confidence,
and that possibly they were eloping together."

"Why did you not arrest him?"

"I had no authority, even if I had had the time.
Although I was ordered to watch the Signor Quadling, I
had no warrant for his arrest. But I decided on the spur
of the moment what course I should take. It seemed to be
the only one, and that was to embark in the same train
and stick close to my man."

"You informed your superiors, I suppose?"

"Pardon me, monsieur," said the Italian blandly to the
Chief, who asked the question, "but have you any right to
inquire into my conduct towards my superiors? In all that
affects the murder I am at your orders, but in this other
matter it is between me and them."

"Ta, ta, ta! They will tell us if you will not. And you
had better be careful, lest you obstruct justice. Speak out,
sir, and beware. What did you intend to do?"

"To act according to circumstances. If my suspicions
were confirmed–"

"What suspicions?"

"Why–that this banker was carrying off any large sum
in cash, notes, securities, as in effect he was."

"Ah! You know that? How?"

"By my own eyes. I looked into his compartment once
and saw him in the act of counting them over, a great
quantity, in fact–"

Again the officials looked at each other significantly. They had got at last to a motive for the crime.

"And that, of course, would have justified his arrest?"

"Exactly. I proposed, directly we arrived in Paris, to claim the assistance of your police and take him into custody. But his fate interposed."

There was a pause, a long pause, for another important point had been reached in the inquiry: the motive for the murder had been made clear, and with it the presumption against the Countess gained terrible strength.

But there was more, perhaps, to be got out of this dark-visaged Italian detective, who had already proved so useful an ally.

"One or two words more," said the Judge to Ripaldi. "During the journey, now, did you have any conversation with this Quadling?"

"None. He kept very much to himself."

"You saw him, I suppose, at the restaurants?"

"Yes, at Modane and Laroche."

"But did not speak to him?"

"Not a word."

"Had he any suspicion, do you think, as to who you were?"

"Why should he? He did not know me. I had taken pains he should never see me."

"Did he speak to any other passenger?"

"Very little. To the Countess. Yes, once or twice, I think, to her maid."

"Ah! that maid. Did you notice her at all? She has not been seen. It is strange. She seems to have disappeared."

"To have run away, in fact?" suggested Ripaldi, with a queer smile.

"Well, at least she is not here with her mistress. Can you offer any explanation of that?"

"She was perhaps afraid. The Countess and she were very good friends, I think. On better, more familiar terms, than is usual between mistress and maid."

"The maid knew something?"

"Ah, monsieur, it is only an idea. But I give it you for what it is worth."

"Well, well, this maid—what was she like?"

"Tall, dark, good-looking, not too reserved. She made other friends—the porter and the English Colonel. I saw the last speaking to her. I spoke to her myself."

"What can have become of her?" said the Judge.

"Would M. le Juge like me to go in search of her? That is, if you have no more questions to ask, no wish to detain me further?"

"We will consider that, and let you know in a moment, if you will wait outside."

And then, when alone, the officials deliberated.

It was a good offer, the man knew her appearance, he was in possession of all the facts, he could be trusted—

"Ah, but can he, though?" queried the detective. "How do we know he has told us truth? What guarantee have we of his loyalty, his good faith? What if he is also concerned in the crime—has some guilty knowledge? What if he killed Quadling himself, or was an accomplice before or after the fact?"

"All these are possibilities, of course, but—pardon me, dear colleague—a little far-fetched, eh?" said the Judge. "Why not utilize this man? If he betrays us—serves us ill— if we had reason to lay hands on him again, he could hardly escape us."

"Let him go, and send someone with him," said the Commissary, the first practical suggestion he had yet made.

"Excellent!" cried the Judge. "You have another man here, Chief; let him go with this Italian."

They called in Ripaldi and told him, "We will accept your services, monsieur, and you can begin your search at once. In what direction do you propose to begin?"

"Where has her mistress gone?"

"How do you know she has gone?"

"At least, she is no longer with us out there. Have you arrested her–or what?"

"No, she is still at large, but we have our eye upon her. She has gone to her hotel–the Madagascar, off the Grands Boulevards."

"Then it is there that I shall look for the maid. No doubt she preceded her mistress to the hotel, or she will join her there very shortly."

"You would not make yourself known, of course? They might give you the slip. You have no authority to detain them, not in France."

"I should take my precautions, and I can always appeal to the police."

"Exactly. That would be your proper course. But you might lose valuable time, a great opportunity, and we wish to guard against that, so we shall associate one of our own people with you in your proceedings."

"Oh! very well, if you wish. It will, no doubt, be best." The Italian readily assented, but a shrewd listener might have guessed from the tone of his voice that the proposal was not exactly pleasing to him.

"I will call in Block," said the Chief, and the second detective inspector appeared to take his instructions.

He was a stout, stumpy little man, with a barrel-like figure, greatly emphasized by the short frock coat he wore; he had smallish pig's eyes buried deep in a fat face, and his round, chubby cheeks hung low over his turned-down collar.

"This gentleman," went on the Chief, indicating Ripaldi, "is a member of the Roman police, and has been so obliging as to offer us his services. You will accompany him, in the first instance, to the Hôtel Madagascar. Put yourself in communication with Galipaud, who is there on duty."

"Would it not be sufficient if I made myself known to M. Galipaud?" suggested the Italian. "I have seen him here, I should recognize him—"

"That is not so certain; he may have changed his appearance. Besides, he does not know the latest developments, and might not be very cordial."

"You might write me a few lines to take to him."

"I think not. We prefer to send Block," replied the Chief, briefly and decidedly. He did not like this pertinacity, and looked at his colleagues as though he sought their concurrence in altering the arrangements for the Italian's mission. It might be wiser to detain him still.

"It was only to save trouble that I made the suggestion," hastily put in Ripaldi. "Naturally I am in your hands. And if I do not meet with the maid at the hotel, I may have to look further, in which case Monsieur—Block? Thank you—would no doubt render valuable assistance."

This speech restored confidence, and a few minutes later the two detectives, already excellent friends from the freemasonry of a common craft, left the station in a closed cab.

9

"What next?" asked the Judge.

"That pestilent English officer, if you please, M. le Juge," said the detective. "That fire-eating, swashbuckling soldier, with his blustering barrack-room ways. I long to come to close quarters with him. He ridiculed me, taunted me, said I knew nothing—we will see, we will see."

"In fact, you wish to interrogate him yourself. Very well. Let us have him in."

When Sir Charles Collingham entered, he included the three officials in one cold, stiff bow, waited a moment, and then, finding he was not offered a chair, said with studied politeness:

"I presume I may sit down?"

"Pardon. Of course; pray be seated," said the Judge, hastily, and evidently a little ashamed of himself.

"Ah! Thanks. Do you object?" went on the General, taking out a silver cigarette-case. "May I offer one?" He handed round the box affably.

"We do not smoke on duty," answered the Chief, rudely. "Nor is smoking permitted in a court of justice."

"Come, come, I wish to show no disrespect. But I cannot recognize this as a court of justice, and I think, if you will forgive me, that I shall take three whiffs. It may help me keep my temper."

He was evidently making game of them. There was no symptom remaining of the recent effervescence when he was acting as the Countess's champion, and he was perfectly—nay, insolently calm and self-possessed.

"You call yourself General Collingham?" went on the Chief.

"I do not call myself. I am General Sir Charles Collingham, of the British Army."

"Retired?"

"No, I am still on the active list."

"These points will have to be verified."

"With all my heart. You have already sent to the British Embassy?"

"Yes, but no one has come," answered the detective, contemptuously.

"If you disbelieve me, why do you question me?"

"It is our duty to question you, and yours to answer. If not, we have means to make you. You are suspected, inculpated in a terrible crime, and your whole attitude is–is–objectionable–unworthy–disgr–"

"Gently, gently, my dear colleague," interposed the Judge. "If you will permit me, I will take up this. And you, M. le Général, I am sure you cannot wish to impede or obstruct us; we represent the law of this country."

"Have I done so, M. le Juge?" answered the General, with the utmost courtesy, as he threw away his half-burned cigarette.

"No, no. I do not imply that in the least. I only entreat you, as a good and gallant gentleman, to meet us in a proper spirit and give us your best help."

"Indeed, I am quite ready. If there has been any unpleasantness, it has surely not been of my making, but rather of that little man there." The General pointed to M. Floçon rather contemptuously, and nearly started a fresh disturbance.

"Well, well, let us say no more of that, and proceed to business. I understand," said the Judge, after fingering a few pages of the dispositions in front of him, "that you are a friend of the Contessa di Castagneto? Indeed, she has told us so herself."

"It was very good of her to call me her friend. I am proud to hear she so considers me."

"How long have you known her?"

"Four or five months. Since the beginning of the last winter season in Rome."

"Did you frequent her house?"

"If you mean, was I permitted to call on her on friendly terms, yes."

"Did you know all her friends?"

"How can I answer that? I know whom I met there from time to time."

"Exactly. Did you often meet among them a Signor—Quadling?"

"Quadling–Quadling? I cannot say that I have. The name is familiar somehow, but I cannot recall the man."

"Have you never heard of the Roman bankers, Correse & Quadling?"

"Ah, of course. Although I have had no dealing with them. Certainly I have never met Mr. Quadling."

"Not at the Countess's?"

"Never–of that I am quite sure."

"And yet we have had positive evidence that he was a constant visitor there."

"It is perfectly incomprehensible to me. Not only have I never met him, but I have never heard the Countess mention his name."

"It will surprise you, then, to be told that he called at her apartment in the Via Margutta on the very evening of her departure from Rome. Called, was admitted, was closeted with her for more than an hour."

"I am surprised, astounded. I called there myself about four in the afternoon to offer my services for the journey, and I too stayed till after five. I can hardly believe it."

"I have more surprises for you, General. What will you think when I tell you that this very Quadling–this friend, acquaintance, call him what you please, but at least intimate enough to pay her a visit on the eve of a long journey–was the man found murdered in the sleeping-car?"

"Can it be possible? Are you sure?" cried Sir Charles, almost starting from his chair. "And what do you deduce from all this? What do you imply? An accusation against that lady? Absurd!"

"I respect your chivalrous desire to stand up for a lady who calls you her friend, but we are officials first, and sentiment cannot be permitted to influence us. We have good reasons for suspecting that lady. I tell you that frankly, and trust to you as a soldier and man of honour not to abuse the confidence reposed in you."

"May I not know those reasons?"

"Because she was in the car–the only woman, you understand–between Laroche and Paris."

"Do you suspect a female hand, then?" asked the General, evidently much interested and impressed.

"That is so, although I am exceeding my duty in revealing this."

"And you are satisfied that this lady, a refined, delicate person in the best society, of the highest character,–believe me, I know that to be the case,–whom you yet suspect of an atrocious crime, was the only female in the car?"

"Obviously. Who else? What other woman could possibly have been in the car? No one got in at Laroche; the train never stopped till it reached Paris."

"On that last point at least you are quite mistaken, I assure you. Why not upon the other also?"

"The train stopped?" interjected the detective. "Why has no one told us that?"

"Possibly because you never asked. But it is nevertheless the fact. Verify it. Everyone will tell you the same."

The detective himself hurried to the door and called in the porter. He was within his rights, of course, but the action showed distrust, at which the General only smiled, but he laughed outright when the still stupid and half-dazed porter, of course, corroborated the statement at once.

"At whose instance was the train pulled up?" asked the detective, and the Judge nodded his head approvingly.

To know that would fix fresh suspicion.

But the porter could not answer the question.

Someone had rung the alarm-bell–so at least the conductor had declared; otherwise they should not have stopped. Yet he, the porter, had not done so, nor did any passenger come forward to admit giving the signal. But there had been a halt. Yes, assuredly.

"This is a new light," the Judge confessed. "Do you draw any conclusion from it?" he went on to ask the General.

"That is surely your business. I have only elicited the fact to disprove your theory. But if you wish, I will tell you how it strikes me."

The Judge bowed assent.

"The bare fact that the train was halted would mean little. That would be the natural act of a timid or excitable person involved indirectly in such a catastrophe. But to disavow the act starts suspicion. The fair inference is that there was some reason, an unavowable reason, for halting the train."

"And that reason would be–"

"You must see it without my assistance, surely! Why, what else but to afford someone an opportunity to leave the car."

"But how could that be? You would have seen that person, some of you, especially at such a critical time. The aisle would be full of people, both exits were thus practically overlooked."

"My idea is–it is only an idea, understand–that the person had already left the car–that is to say, the interior of the car."

"Escaped how? Where? What do you mean?"

"Escaped through the open window of the compartment where you found the murdered man."

"You noticed the open window, then?" quickly asked the detective. "When was that?"

"Directly I entered the compartment at the first alarm. It occurred to me at once that someone might have gone through it."

"But no woman could have done it. To climb out of an express train going at top speed would be an impossible feat for a woman," said the detective, doggedly.

"Why, in God's name, do you still harp upon the woman? Why should it be a woman more than a man?"

"Because"–it was the Judge who spoke, but he paused a moment in deference to a gesture of protest from M. Floçon. The little detective was much concerned at the utter want of reticence displayed by his colleague.

"Because," went on the Judge with decision–"because this was found in the compartment;" and he held out the piece of lace and the scrap of beading for the General's inspection, adding quickly, "You have seen these, or one of them, or something like them before. I am sure of it; I call upon you; I demand–no, I appeal to your sense of honour, Sir Collingham. Tell me, please, exactly what you know."

10

The General sat for a time staring hard at the bit of torn lace and the broken beads. Then he spoke out firmly:

"It is my duty to withhold nothing. It is not the lace. That I could not swear to; for me—and probably for most men—two pieces of lace are very much the same. But I think I have seen these beads, or something exactly like them, before."

"Where? When?"

"They formed part of the trimming of a mantle worn by the Contessa di Castagneto."

"Ah!" it was the same interjection uttered simultaneously by the three Frenchmen, but each had a very different note; in the Judge it was deep interest, in the detective triumph, in the Commissary indignation, as when he caught a criminal red-handed.

"Did she wear it on the journey?" continued the Judge.

"As to that I cannot say."

"Come, come, General, you were with her constantly; you must be able to tell us. We insist on being told." This fiercely, from the now jubilant M. Floçon.

"I repeat that I cannot say. To the best of my recollection, the Countess wore a long travelling cloak—an ulster, as we call them. The jacket with those bead ornaments may have been underneath. But if I have seen them,—as I believe I have,—it was not during this journey."

Here the Judge whispered to M. Floçon, "The searcher did not discover any second mantle."

"How do we know the woman examined thoroughly?" he replied. "Here, at least, is direct evidence as to the beads. At last the net is drawing round this fine Countess."

"Well, at any rate," said the detective aloud, returning to the General, "these beads were found in the compartment of the murdered man. I should like that explained, please."

"By me? How can I explain it? And the fact does not bear upon what we were considering, as to whether any one had left the car."

"Why not?"

"The Countess, as we know, never left the car. As to her entering this particular compartment,–at any previous time,–it is highly improbable. Indeed, it is rather insulting her to suggest it."

"She and this Quadling were close friends."

"So you say. On what evidence I do not know, but I dispute it."

"Then how could the beads get there? They were her property, worn by her."

"Once, I admit, but not necessarily on this journey. Suppose she had given the mantle away–to her maid, for instance; I believe ladies often pass on their things to their maids."

"It is all pure presumption, a mere theory. This maid– she has not as yet been imported into the discussion."

"Then I would suggest that you do so without delay. She is to my mind a–well, rather a curious person."

"You know her–spoke to her?"

"I know her, in a way. I had seen her in the Via Margutta, and I nodded to her when she came first into the car."

"And on the journey–you spoke to her frequently?"

"I? Oh, dear, no, not at all. I noticed her, certainly; I could not help it, and perhaps I ought to tell her mistress. She seemed to make friends a little too readily with people."

"As for instance–?"

"With the porter to begin with. I saw them together at Laroche, in the buffet at the bar; and that Italian, the man who was in here before me; indeed, with the murdered man. She seemed to know them all."

"Do you imply that the maid might be of use in this inquiry?"

"Most assuredly I do. As I tell you, she was constantly in and out of the car, and more or less intimate with several of the passengers."

"Including her mistress, the Countess," put in M. Floçon. The General laughed pleasantly.

"Most ladies are, I presume, on intimate terms with their maids. They say no man is a hero to his valet. It is the same, I suppose, with the other sex."

"So intimate," went on the little detective, with much malicious emphasis, "that now the maid has disappeared lest she might be asked inconvenient questions about her mistress."

"Disappeared? You are sure?"

"She cannot be found, that is all we know."

"It is as I thought, then. She it was who left the car!" cried Sir Charles, with so much vehemence that the officials were startled out of their dignified reserve, and shouted back almost in a breath: "Explain yourself. Quick, quick. What in God's name do you mean?"

"I had my suspicions from the first, and I will tell you why. At Laroche the car emptied, as you may have heard; everyone except the Countess, at least, went over to the restaurant for early coffee; I with the rest. I was one of the first to finish, and I strolled back to the platform to get a few whiffs of a cigarette. At that moment I saw, or thought I saw, the end of a skirt disappearing into the sleeping-car. I concluded it was this maid, Hortense, who was taking her mistress a cup of coffee. Then my brother came up, we exchanged a few words, and entered the car together."

"By the same door as that through which you had seen the skirt pass?"

"No, by the other. My brother went back to his berth, but I paused in the corridor to finish my cigarette after the train had gone on. By this time everyone but myself had returned to his berth, and I was on the point of lying down again for half an hour, when I distinctly heard the handle turned of the compartment I knew to be vacant all through the run."

"That was the one with berths 11 and 12?"

"Probably. It was next to the Countess. Not only was the handle turned, but the door partly opened—"

"It was not the porter?"

"Oh, no, he was in his seat,—you know it, at the end of the car,—sound asleep, snoring; I could hear him."

"Did any one come out of the vacant compartment?"

"No; but I was almost certain, I believe I could swear that I saw the same skirt, just the hem of it, a black skirt, sway forward beyond the door, just for a second. Then all at once the door was closed again fast."

"What did you conclude from this? Or did you think nothing of it?"

"I thought very little. I supposed it was that the maid wished to be near her mistress as we were approaching Paris, and I had heard from the Countess that the porter had made many difficulties. But you see, after what has happened, that there was a reason for stopping the train."

"Quite so," M. Floçon readily admitted, with a scarcely concealed sneer.

He had quite made up his mind now that it was the Countess who had rung the alarm-bell, in order to allow of the escape of the maid, her confederate and accomplice.

"And you still have an impression that someone—presumably this woman—got off the car, somehow, during the stoppage?" he asked.

"I suggest it, certainly. Whether it was or could be so, I must leave to your superior judgment."

"What! A woman climb out like that? Bah! Tell that to someone else!"

"You have, of course, examined the exterior of the car, dear colleague?" now said the Judge.

"Assuredly, once, but I will do it again. Still, the outside is quite smooth, there is no foot-board. Only an acrobat could succeed in thus escaping, and then only at the peril of his life. But a woman—oh, no! it is too absurd."

"With help she might, I think, get up on to the roof," quickly remarked Sir Charles. "I have looked out of the window of my compartment. It would be nothing for a man, nor much for a woman if assisted."

"That we will see for ourselves," said the detective, ungraciously.

"The sooner the better," added the Judge, and the whole party rose from their chairs, intending to go straight to the car, when the policeman on guard appeared at the door, followed close by an English military officer in uniform, whom he was trying to keep back, but with no great success. It was Colonel Papillon of the Embassy.

"Halloa, Jack! you are a good chap," cried the General, quickly going forward to shake hands. "I was sure you would come."

"Come, sir! Of course I came. I was just going to an official function, as you see, but his Excellency insisted, my horse was at the door, and here I am."

All this was in English, but the attaché turned now to the officials, and, with many apologies for his intrusion, suggested that they should allow his friend, the General, to return with him to the Embassy when they had done with him.

"Of course we will answer for him. He shall remain at your disposal, and will appear whenever called upon." He returned to Sir Charles, asking, "You will promise that, sir?"

"Oh, willingly. I had always meant to stay on a bit in Paris. And really I should like to see the end of this. But my brother? He must get home for next Sunday's duty.

He has nothing to tell, but he would come back to Paris at any time if his evidence was wanted."

The French Judge very obligingly agreed to all these proposals, and two more of the detained passengers, making four in all, now left the station.

Then the officials proceeded to the car, which still remained as the Chief Detective had left it.

Here they soon found how just were the General's previsions.

11

The three officials went straight to where the still open window showed the particular spot to be examined. The exterior of the car was a little smirched and stained with the dust of the journey, lying thick in parts, and in others there were a few great splotches of mud plastered on.

The detective paused for a moment to get a general view, looking, in the light of the General's suggestion, for either hand or foot marks, anything like a trace of the passage of a feminine skirt, across the dusty surface.

But nothing was to be seen, nothing definite or conclusive at least. Only here and there a few lines and scratches that might be encouraging, but proved little.

Then the Commissary, drawing nearer, called attention to some suspicious spots sprinkled about the window, but above it towards the roof.

"What is it?" asked the detective, as his colleague with the point of his long fore-finger nail picked at the thin crust on the top of one of these spots, disclosing a dark, viscous core.

"I could not swear to it, but I believe it is blood."

"Blood! Good Heavens!" cried the detective, as he dragged his powerful magnifying glass out of his pocket and applied it to the spot. "Look, M. le Juge," he added, after a long and minute examination. "What say you?"

"It has that appearance. Only medical evidence can positively decide, but I believe it is blood."

"Now we are on the right track, I feel convinced. Someone fetch a ladder."

One of these curious French ladders, narrow at the top, splayed out at the base, was quickly leaned against the car, and the detective ran up, using his magnifier as he climbed.

"There is more here, much more, and something like— yes, beyond question it is–the print of two hands upon the roof. It was here she climbed."

"No doubt. I can see it now exactly. She would sit on the window ledge, the lower limbs inside the car here and held there. Then with her hands she would draw herself up to the roof," said the Judge.

"But what nerve! what strength of arm!"

"It was life and death. Within the car was more terrible danger. Fear will do much in such a case. We all know that. Well! what more?"

By this time the detective had stepped on to the roof of the car.

"More, more, much more! Footprints, as plain as a picture. A woman's feet. Wait, let me follow them to the end," said he, cautiously creeping forward to the end of the car.

A minute or two more, and he rejoined his colleagues on the ground level, and, rubbing his hands, declared joyously that it was all perfectly clear.

"Dangerous or not, difficult or not, she did it. I have traced her; have seen where she must have lain crouching ever so long, followed her all along the top of the car, to the end where she got down above the little platform exit. Beyond doubt she left the car when it stopped, and by arrangement with her confederate."

"The Countess?"

"Who else?"

"And at a point near Paris. The English General said the halt was within twenty minutes' run of the station."

"Then it is from that point we must commence our search for her. The Italian has gone on the wrong scent."

"Not necessarily. The maid, we may be sure, will try to communicate with her mistress."

"Still, it would be well to secure her before she can do that," said the Judge. "With all we know now, a sharp interrogation might extract some very damaging admissions from her," went on the detective, eagerly. "Who is to go? I have sent away both my assistants. Of course I can telephone for another man, or I might go myself."

"No, no, dear colleague, we cannot spare you just yet. Telephone by all means. I presume you would wish to be present at the rest of the interrogatories?"

"Certainly, you are right. We may elicit more about this maid. Let us call in the porter now. He is said to have had relations with her. Something more may be got out of him."

The more did not amount to much. Groote, the porter, came in, cringing and wretched, in the abject state of a man who has lately been drugged and is now slowly recovering. Although sharply questioned, he had nothing to add to his first story.

"Speak out," said the Judge, harshly. "Tell us everything plainly and promptly, or I shall send you straight to gaol. The order is already made out;" and as he spoke, he waved a flimsy bit of paper before him.

"I know nothing," the porter protested, piteously.

"That is false. We are fully informed and no fools. We are certain that no such catastrophe could have occurred without your knowledge or connivance."

"Indeed, gentlemen, indeed–"

"You were drinking with this maid at the buffet at Laroche. You had more drink with her, or from her hands, afterwards in the car."

"No, gentlemen, that is not so. I could not–she was not in the car."

"We know better. You cannot deceive us. You were her accomplice, and the accomplice of her mistress, also, I have no doubt."

"I declare solemnly that I am quite innocent of all this. I hardly remember what happened at Laroche or after. I do not deny the drink at the buffet. It was very

nasty, I thought, and could not tell why, nor why I could
not hold my head up when I got back to the car."

"You went off to sleep at once? Is that what you
pretend?"

"It must have been so. Yes. Then I know nothing
more, not till I was aroused."

And beyond this, a tale to which he stuck with
undeviating persistence, they could elicit nothing.

"He is either too clever for us or an absolute idiot and
fool," said the Judge, wearily, at last, when Groote had
gone out. "We had better commit him to Mazas and hold
him there in solitary confinement under our hands. After
a day or two of that he may be less difficult."

"It is quite clear he was drugged, that the maid put
opium or laudanum into his drink at Laroche."

"And enough of it apparently, for he says he went off
to sleep directly he returned to the car," the Judge
remarked.

"He says so. But he must have had a second dose, or
why was the vial found on the ground by his seat?" asked
the Chief, thoughtfully, as much of himself as of the
others.

"I cannot believe in a second dose. How was it
administered—by whom? It was laudanum, and could only
be given in a drink. He says he had no second drink. And
by whom? The maid? He says he did not see the maid
again."

"Pardon me, M. le Juge, but do you not give too much
credibility to the porter? For me, his evidence is tainted,
and I hardly believe a word of it. Did he not tell me at
first he had not seen this maid after Amberieux at 8
P.M.? Now he admits that he was drinking with her at
the buffet at Laroche. It is all a tissue of lies, his losing
the pocket-book and his papers too. There is something to
conceal. Even his sleepiness, his stupidity, are likely to
have been assumed."

"I do not think he is acting; he has not the ability to
deceive us like that."

"Well, then, what if the Countess took him the second drink?"

"Oh! oh! That is the purest conjecture. There is nothing whatever to suggest or support that."

"Then how explain the finding of the vial near the porter's seat?"

"May it not have been dropped there on purpose?" put in the Commissary, with another flash of intelligence.

"On purpose?" queried the detective, crossly, foreseeing an answer that would not please him.

"On purpose to bring suspicion on the lady?"

"I don't see it in that light. That would imply that she was not in the plot, and plot there certainly was; everything points to it. The drugging, the open window, the maid's escape."

"A plot, no doubt, but organized by whom? These two women only? Could either of them have struck the fatal blow? Hardly. Women have the wit to conceive, but neither courage nor brute force to execute. There was a man in this, rest assured."

"Granted. But who? That fire-eating Sir Collingham?" quickly asked the detective, giving rein once more to his hatred.

"That is not a solution that commends itself to me, I must confess," declared the Judge. "The General's conduct has been blameworthy and injudicious, but he is not of the stuff that makes criminals."

"Who, then? The porter? No? The clergyman? No? The French gentlemen?–well, we have not examined them yet; but from what I saw at the first cursory glance, I am not disposed to suspect them."

"What of that Italian?" asked the Commissary.

"Are you sure of him? His looks did not please me greatly, and he was very eager to get away from here. What if he takes to his heels?"

"Block is with him," the Chief put in hastily, with the evident desire to stifle an unpleasant misgiving. "We have touch of him if we want him, as we may."

How much they might want him they only realized when they got further in their inquiry!

12

Only the two Frenchmen remained for examination. They had been left to the last by pure accident. The exigencies of the inquiry had led to the preference of others, but these two well-broken and submissive gentlemen made no visible protest. However much they may have chafed inwardly at the delay, they knew better than to object; any outburst of discontent would, they knew, recoil on themselves. Not only were they perfectly patient now when summoned before the officers of justice, they were most eager to give every assistance to the law, to go beyond the mere letter, and, if needs be, volunteer information.

The first called in was the elder, M. Anatole Lafolay, a true Parisian *bourgeois*, fat and comfortable, unctuous in speech, and exceedingly deferential.

The story he told was in its main outlines that which we already know, but he was further questioned, by the light of the latest facts and ideas as now elicited.

The line adroitly taken by the Judge was to get some evidence of collusion and combination among the passengers, especially with reference to two of them, the two women of the party. On this important point M. Lafolay had something to say.

Asked if he had seen or noticed the lady's maid on the journey, he answered "yes" very decisively and with a smack of the lips, as though the sight of this pretty and attractive person had given him considerable satisfaction.

"Did you speak to her?"

"Oh, no. I had no opportunity. Besides, she had her own friends– great friends, I fancy. I caught her more than once whispering in the corner of the car with one of them."

"And that was–?"

"I think the Italian gentleman; I am almost sure I recognized his clothes. I did not see his face, it was turned from me–towards hers, and very close, I may be permitted to say."

"And they were friendly?"

"More than friendly, I should say. Very intimate indeed. I should not have been surprised if–when I turned away as a matter of fact–if he did not touch, just touch, her red lips. It would have been excusable–forgive me, messieurs."

"Aha! They were so intimate as that? Indeed! And did she reserve her favours exclusively for him? Did no one else address her, pay her court on the quiet–you understand?"

"I saw her with the porter, I believe, at Laroche, but only then. No, the Italian was her chief companion."

"Did anyone else notice the flirtation, do you think?"

"Possibly. There was no secrecy. It was very marked. We could all see."

"And her mistress too?"

"That I will not say. The lady I saw but little during the journey."

A few more questions, mainly personal, as to his address, business, probable presence in Paris for the next few weeks, and M. Lafolay was permitted to depart.

The examination of the younger Frenchman, a smart, alert young man, of pleasant, insinuating address, with a quick, inquisitive eye, followed the same lines, and was distinctly corroborative on all the points to which M. Lafolay spoke. But M. Jules Devaux had something startling to impart concerning the Countess.

When asked if he had seen her or spoken to her, he shook his head.

"No; she kept very much to herself," he said. "I saw her but little, hardly at all, except at Modane. She kept her own berth."

"Where she received her own friends?"

"Oh, beyond doubt. The Englishmen both visited her there, but not the Italian."

"The Italian? Are we to infer that she knew the Italian?"

"That is what I wish to convey. Not on the journey, though. Between Rome and Paris she did not seem to know him. It was afterwards; this morning, in fact, that I came to the conclusion that there was some secret understanding between them."

"Why do you say that, M. Devaux?" cried the detective, excitedly. "Let me urge you and implore you to speak out, and fully. This is of the utmost, of the very first, importance."

"Well, gentlemen, I will tell you. As you are well aware, on arrival at this station we were all ordered to leave the car, and marched to the waiting-room, out there. As a matter of course, the lady entered first, and she was seated when I went in. There was a strong light on her face."

"Was her veil down?"

"Not then. I saw her lower it later, and, as I think, for reasons I will presently put before you. Madame has a beautiful face, and I gazed at it with sympathy, grieving for her, in fact, in such a trying situation; when suddenly I saw a great and remarkable change come over it."

"Of what character?"

"It was a look of horror, disgust, surprise,—a little perhaps of all three; I could not quite say which, it faded so quickly and was followed by a cold, deathlike pallor. Then almost immediately she lowered her veil."

"Could you form any explanation for what you saw in her face? What caused it?"

"Something unexpected, I believe, some shock, or the sight of something shocking. That was how it struck me, and so forcibly that I turned to look over my shoulder, expecting to find the reason there. And it was."

"That reason—?"

"Was the entrance of the Italian, who came just behind me. I am certain of this; he almost told me so himself, not in words, but the mistakable leer he gave her in reply. It was wicked, sardonic, devilish, and proved beyond doubt that there was some secret, some guilty secret perhaps, between them."

"And was that all?" cried both the Judge and M. Floçon in a breath, leaning forward in their eagerness to hear more.

"For the moment, yes. But I was made so interested, so suspicious by this, that I watched the Italian closely, awaiting, expecting further developments. They were long in coming; indeed, I am only at the end now."

"Explain, pray, as quickly as possible, and in your own words."

"It was like this, monsieur. When we were all seated, I looked round, and did not at first see our Italian. At last I discovered he had taken a back seat, through modesty perhaps, or to be out of observation–how was I to know? He sat in the shadow by a door, that, in fact, which leads into this room. He was thus in the background, rather out of the way, but I could see his eyes glittering in that far-off corner, and they were turned in our direction, always fixed upon the lady, you understand. She was next me, the whole time.

"Then, as you will remember, monsieur, you called us in one by one, and I, with M. Lafolay, was the first to appear before you. When I returned to the outer room, the Italian was still staring, but not so fixedly or continuously, at the lady. From time to time his eyes wandered towards a table near which he sat, and which was just in the gangway or passage by which people must pass into your presence.

"There was some reason for this, I felt sure, although I did not understand it immediately.

"Presently I got at the hidden meaning There was a small piece of paper, rolled up or crumpled up into a ball, lying upon this table, and the Italian wished, nay, was desperately anxious, to call the lady's attention to it. If I had had any doubt of this, it was quite removed after the man had gone into the inner room. As he left us, he turned his head over his shoulder significantly and nodded very slightly, but still perceptibly, at the ball of paper.

"Well, gentlemen, I was now satisfied in my own mind that this was some artful attempt of his to communicate with the lady, and had she fallen in with it, I should have immediately informed you, the proper authorities. But whether from stupidity, dread, disinclination, a direct, definite refusal to have any dealings with this man, the lady would not—at any rate did not—pick up the ball, as she might have done easily when she in her turn passed the table on her way to your presence.

"I have no doubt it was thrown there for her, and probably you will agree with me. But it takes two to make a game of this sort, and the lady would not join. Neither on leaving the room nor on returning would she take up the missive."

"And what became of it, then?" asked the detective in breathless excitement. "I have it here." M. Devaux opened the palm of his hand and displayed the scrap of paper in the hollow rolled up into a small tight ball.

"When and how did you become possessed of it?"

"I got it only just now, when I was called in here. Before that I could not move. I was tied to my chair, practically, and ordered strictly not to move."

"Perfectly. Monsieur's conduct has been admirable. And now tell us—what does it contain? Have you looked at it?"

"By no means. It is just as I picked it up. Will you gentlemen take it, and if you think fit, tell me what is there? Some writing—a message of some sort, or I am greatly mistaken."

"Yes, here are words written in pencil," said the detective, unrolling the paper, which he handed on to the Judge, who read the contents aloud–

"Be careful. Say nothing. If you betray me, you will be lost too."

A long silence followed, broken first by the Judge, who said at last solemnly to Devaux:

"Monsieur, in the name of justice I beg to thank you most warmly. You have acted with admirable tact and judgment, and have rendered us invaluable assistance. Have you anything further to tell us?"

"No, gentlemen. That is all. And you–you have no more questions to ask? Then I presume I may withdraw?"

Beyond doubt it had been reserved for the last witness to produce facts that constituted the very essence of the inquiry.

13

The examination was now over, and, the dispositions having been drawn up and signed, the investigating officials remained for some time in conference.

"It lies with those three, of course–the two women and the Italian. They are jointly, conjointly concerned, although the exact degrees of guilt cannot quite be apportioned," said the detective.

"And all three are at large!" added the Judge.

"If you will issue warrants for arrest, M. le Juge, we can take them–two of them at any rate–when we choose."

"That should be at once," remarked the Commissary, eager, as usual, for decisive action.

"Very well. Let us proceed in that way. Prepare the warrants," said the Judge, turning to his clerk. "And you," he went on, addressing M. Floçon, "dear colleague, will you see to their execution? Madame is at the Hôtel Madagascar; that will be easy. The Italian Ripaldi we shall hear of through your inspector Block. As for the maid, Hortense Petitpré, we must search for her. That too, sir, you will of course undertake?"

"I will charge myself with it, certainly. My man should be here by now, and I will instruct him at once. Ask for him," said M. Floçon to the guard whom he called in.

"The inspector is there," said the guard, pointing to the outer room. "He has just returned."

"Returned? You mean arrived."

"No, monsieur, returned. It is Block, who left an hour or more ago."

"Block? Then something has happened–he has some special information, some great news! Shall we see him, M. le Juge?"

When Block appeared, it was evident that something had gone wrong with him. His face wore a look of hot, flurried excitement, and his manner was one of abject, cringing self-abasement.

"What is it?" asked the little Chief, sharply. "You are alone. Where is your man?"

"Alas, monsieur! how shall I tell you? He has gone—disappeared! I have lost him!"

"Impossible! You cannot mean it! Gone, now, just when we most want him? Never!"

"It is so, unhappily."

"Idiot! *Triple* idiot! You shall be dismissed, discharged from this hour. You are a disgrace to the force." M. Floçon raved furiously at his abashed subordinate, blaming him a little too harshly and unfairly, forgetting that until quite recently there had been no strong suspicion against the Italian. We are apt at times to expect others to be intuitively possessed of knowledge that has only come to us at a much later date.

"How was it? Explain. Of course you have been drinking. It is that, or your great gluttony. You were beguiled into some eating-house."

"Monsieur, you shall hear the exact truth. When we started more than an hour ago, our fiacre took the usual route, by the Quais and along the riverside. My gentleman made himself most pleasant"

"No doubt," growled the Chief.

"Offered me an excellent cigar, and talked—not about the affair, you understand—but of Paris, the theatres, the races, Longchamps, Auteuil, the grand restaurants. He knew everything, all Paris, like his pocket. I was much surprised, but he told me his business often brought him here. He had been employed to follow up several great Italian criminals, and had made a number of important arrests in Paris."

"Get on, get on! come to the essential."

"Well, in the middle of the journey, when we were about the Pont Henri Quatre, he said, 'Figure to yourself, my friend, that it is now near noon, that nothing has passed my lips since before daylight at Laroche. What say you? Could you eat a mouthful, just a scrap on the thumb-nail? Could you?'"

"And you–greedy, gormandizing beast!–you agreed?"

"My faith, monsieur, I too was hungry. It was my regular hour. Well–at any rate, for my sins I accepted. We entered the first restaurant, that of the 'Reunited Friends,' you know it, perhaps, monsieur? A good house, especially noted for tripe *à la mode de Caen*." In spite of his anguish, Block smacked his fat lips at the thought of this most succulent but very greasy dish.

"How often must I tell you to get on?"

"Forgive me, monsieur, but it is all part of my story. We had oysters, two dozen Marennes, and a glass or two of Chablis; then a good portion of tripe, and with them a bottle, only one, monsieur, of Pontet Canet; after that a beefsteak with potatoes and a little Burgundy, then a rum omelet."

"Great Heavens! you should be the fat man in a fair, not an agent of the Detective Bureau."

"It was all this that helped me to my destruction. He ate, this devilish Italian, like three, and I too, I was so hungry,–forgive me, sir,–I did my share. But by the time we reached the cheese, a fine, ripe Camembert, had our coffee, and one thimbleful of green Chartreuse, I was *plein jusqu'au bec*, gorged up to the beak."

"And what of your duty, your service, pray?"

"I did think of it, monsieur, but then, he, the Italian, was just the same as myself. He was a colleague. I had no fear of him, not till the very last, when he played me this evil turn. I suspected nothing when he brought out his pocketbook,–it was stuffed full, monsieur; I saw that and my confidence increased,–called for the reckoning, and paid with an Italian bank-note. The waiter looked doubtful at the foreign money, and went out to consult the manager. A minute after, my man got up, saying:

"'There may be some trouble about changing that bank-note. Excuse me one moment, pray.' He went out, monsieur, and piff-paff, he was no more to be seen."

"Ah, *nigaud* (ass), you are too foolish to live! Why did you not follow him? Why let him out of your sight?"

"But, monsieur, I was not to know, was I? I was to accompany him, not to watch him. I have done wrong, I confess. But then, who was to tell he meant to run away?"

M. Floçon could not deny the justice of this defence. It was only now, at the eleventh hour, that the Italian had become inculpated, and the question of his possible anxiety to escape had never been considered.

"He was so artful," went on Block in further extenuation of his offence. "He left everything behind. His overcoat, stick, this book—his own private memorandum-book seemingly—" "Book? Hand it me," said the Chief, and when it came into his hands he began to turn over the leaves hurriedly. It was a small brass-bound note-book or diary, and was full of close writing in pencil.

"I do not understand, not more than a word here and there. It is no doubt Italian. Do you know that language, M. le Juge?"

"Not perfectly, but I can read it. Allow me."

He also turned over the pages, pausing to read a passage here and there, and nodding his head from time to time, evidently struck with the importance of the matter recorded.

Meanwhile, M. Floçon continued an angry conversation with his offending subordinate.

"You will have to find him, Block, and that speedily, within twenty-four hours,—to-day, indeed,—or I will break you like a stick, and send you into the gutter. Of course, such a consummate ass as you have proved yourself would not think of searching the restaurant or the immediate neighbourhood, or of making inquiries as to whether he had been seen, or as to which way he had gone?"

"Pardon me, monsieur is too hard on me. I have been unfortunate, a victim to circumstances, still I believe I know my duty. Yes, I made inquiries, and, what is more, I heard of him."

"Where? how?" asked the Chief, gruffly, but obviously much interested.

"He never spoke to the manager, but walked out and let the change go. It was a note for a hundred *lire*, a hundred francs, and the restaurant bill was no more than seventeen francs."

"Hah! That is greatly against him indeed."

"He was much pressed, in a great hurry. Directly he crossed the threshold he called the first cab and was driving away, but he was stopped—"

"The devil! Why did they not keep him, then?"

"Stopped, but only for a moment, and accosted by a woman."

"A woman?"

"Yes, monsieur. They exchanged but three words. He wished to pass on, to leave her, she would not consent, then they both got into the cab and were driven away together."

The officials were now listening with all ears.

"Tell me," said the Chief, "quick, this woman—what was she like? Did you get her description?"

"Tall, slight, well formed, dressed all in black. Her face—it was a policeman who saw her, and he said she was good-looking, dark, brunette, black hair."

"It is the maid herself!" cried the little Chief, springing up and slapping his thigh in exuberant glee. "The maid! The missing maid!"

14

The joy of the Chief of Detectives at having thus come, as he supposed, upon the track of the missing maid, Hortense Petitpré, was somewhat dashed by the doubts freely expressed by the Judge as to the result of any search. Since Block's return, M. Beaumont le Hardi had developed strong symptoms of discontent and disapproval at his colleague's proceedings.

"But if it was this Hortense Petitpré how did she get there, by the bridge Henri Quatre, when we thought to find her somewhere down the line? It cannot be the same woman."

"I beg your pardon, gentlemen," interposed Block. "May I say one word? I believe I can supply some interesting information about Hortense Petitpré. I understand that someone like her was seen here in the station not more than an hour ago."

" *Peste!* Why were we not told this sooner?" cried the Chief, impetuously.

"Who saw her? Did he speak to her? Call him in; let us see how much he knows."

The man was summoned, one of the subordinate railway officials, who made a specific report.

Yes, he had seen a tall, slight, neat-looking woman, dressed entirely in black, who, according to her account, had arrived at 10.30 by the slow local train from Dijon.

"*Fichtre!*" said the Chief, angrily; "and this is the first we have heard of it."

"Monsieur was much occupied at the time, and, indeed, then we had not heard of your inquiry."

"I notified the station-master quite early, two or three hours since, about 9 A.M. This is most exasperating!"

"Instructions to look out for this woman have only just reached us, monsieur. There were certain formalities, I suppose."

For once the detective cursed in his heart the red-tape, roundabout ways of French officialism.

"Well, well! Tell me about her," he said, with a resignation he did not feel. "Who saw her?"

"I, monsieur. I spoke to her myself. She was on the outside of the station, alone, unprotected, in a state of agitation and alarm. I went up and offered my services. Then she told me she had come from Dijon, that friends who were to have met her had not appeared. I suggested that I should put her into a cab and send her to her destination. But she was afraid of losing her friends, and preferred to wait."

"A fine story! Did she appear to know what had happened? Had she heard of the murder?"

"Something, monsieur."

"Who could have told her? Did you?"

"No, not I. But she knew."

"Was not that in itself suspicious? The fact has not yet been made public."

"It was in the air, monsieur. There was a general impression that something had happened. That was to be seen on every face, in the whispered talk, the movement to and fro of the police and the guards."

"Did she speak of it, or refer to it?"

"Only to ask if the murderer was known; whether the passengers had been detained; whether there was any inquiry in progress; and then—"

"What then?"

"This gentleman," pointing to Block, "came out, accompanied by another. They passed pretty close to us, and I noticed that the lady slipped quickly on one side."

"She recognized her confederate, of course, but did not wish to be seen just then. Did he, the person with Block here, see her?"

"Hardly, I think; it was all so quick, and they were gone, in a minute, to the cab-stand."

"What did your woman do?"

"She seemed to have changed her mind all at once, and declared she would not wait for her friends. Now she was in quite a hurry to go."

"Of course! and left you like a fool planted there. I suppose she took a cab and followed the others, Block here and his companion."

"I believe she did. I saw her cab close behind theirs."

"It is too late to lament this now," said the Chief, after a short pause, looking at his colleagues. "At least it confirms our ideas, and brings us to certain definite conclusions. We must lay hands on these two. Their guilt is all but established. Their own acts condemn them. They must be arrested without a moment's delay."

"If you can find them!" suggested the Judge, with a very perceptible sneer.

"That we shall certainly do. Trust to Block, who is very nearly concerned. His future depends on his success. You quite understand that, my man?"

Block made a gesture half-deprecating, half-confident.

"I do not despair, gentlemen; and if I might make so bold, sir, I will ask you to assist? If you would give orders direct from the Prefecture to make the round of the cab-stands, to ask of all the agents in charge the information we need? Before night we shall have heard from the cabman who drove them what became of this couple, and so get our birds themselves, or a point of fresh departure."

"And you, Block, where shall you go?"

"Where I left him, or rather where he left me," replied the inspector, with an attempt at wit, which fell quite flat, being extinguished by a frigid look from the Judge.

"Go," said M. Floçon, briefly and severely, to his subordinate; "and remember that you have now to justify your retention on the force."

Then, turning to M. Beaumont le Hardi, the Chief went on pleasantly:

"Well, M. le Juge, it promises, I think; it is all fairly satisfactory, eh?"

"I am sorry I cannot agree with you," replied the Judge, harshly. "On the contrary, I consider that we–or more exactly you, for neither I nor M. Garraud accept any share in it–you have so far failed, and miserably."

"Your pardon, M. le Juge, you are too severe," protested M. Floçon, quite humbly.

"Well! Look at it from all points of view. What have we got? What have we gained? Nothing, or, if anything, it is of the smallest, and it is already jeopardized, if not absolutely lost."

"We have at least gained the positive assurance of the guilt of certain individuals."

"Whom you have allowed to slip through your fingers."

"Ah, not so, M. le Juge! We have one under surveillance. My man Galipaud is there at the hotel watching the Countess."

"Do not talk to me of your men, M. Floçon," angrily interposed the Judge. "One of them has given us a touch of his quality. Why should not the other be equally foolish? I quite expect to hear that the Countess also has gone, that would be the climax!"

"It shall not happen. I will take the warrant and arrest her now, at once, myself," cried M. Floçon.

"Well, that will be something, yet not much. Yes, she is only one, and not to my mind the most criminal. We do not know as yet the exact responsibility of each, the exact measure of their guilt; but I do not myself believe that the Countess was a prime mover, or, indeed, more than an accessory. She was drawn into it, perhaps involved, how or why we cannot know, but possibly by fortuitous circumstances that put an unavoidable pressure upon her; a consenting party, but under protest. That is my view of the lady."

M. Floçon shook his head. Prepossessions with him were tenacious, and he had made up his mind about the Countess's guilt.

"When you again interrogate her, M. le Juge, by the light of your present knowledge, I believe you will think otherwise. She will confess,—you will make her, your skill is unrivalled,—and you will then admit, M. le Juge, that I was right in my suspicions."

"Ah, well, produce her! We shall see," said the Judge, somewhat mollified by M. Floçon's fulsome flattery.

"I will bring her to your chamber of instruction within an hour, M. le Juge," said the detective, very confidently.

But he was doomed to disappointment in this as he was in other respects.

15

Let us go back a little in point of time, and follow the movements of Sir Charles Collingham.

It was barely 11 A.M. when he left the Lyons Station with his brother, the Reverend Silas, and the military attaché, Colonel Papillon. They paused for a moment outside the station while the baggage was being got together.

"See, Silas," said the General, pointing to the clock, "you will have plenty of time for the 11.50 train to Calais for London, but you must hurry up and drive straight across Paris to the Nord. I suppose he can go, Jack?"

"Certainly, as he has promised to return if called upon."

And Mr. Collingham promptly took advantage of the permission.

"But you, General, what are your plans?" went on the attaché.

"I shall go to the club first, get a room, dress, and all that. Then call at the Hôtel Madagascar. There is a lady there,—one of our party, in fact,—and I should like to ask after her. She may be glad of my services."

"English? Is there anything we can do for her?"

"Yes, she is an Englishwoman, but the widow of an Italian—the Contessa di Castagneto."

"Oh, but I know her!" said Papillon. "I remember her in Rome two or three years ago. A deuced pretty woman, very much admired, but she was in deep mourning then, and went out very little. I wished she had gone out more. There were lots of men ready to fall at her feet."

"You were in Rome, then, some time back? Did you ever come across a man there, Quadling, the banker?"

"Of course I did. Constantly. He was a good deal about—a rather free-living, self-indulgent sort of chap. And now you mention his name, I recollect they said he was much smitten by this particular lady, the Contessa di Castagneto."

"And did she encourage him?"

"Lord! how can I tell? Who shall say how a woman's fancy falls? It might have suited her too. They said she was not in very good circumstances, and he was thought to be a rich man. Of course we know better than that now."

"Why *now*?"

"Haven't you heard? It was in the *Figaro* yesterday, and in all the Paris papers. Quadling's bank has gone to smash; he has bolted with all the 'ready' he could lay hands upon."

"He didn't get far, then!" cried Sir Charles. "You look surprised, Jack. Didn't they tell you? This Quadling was the man murdered in the sleeping-car. It was no doubt for the money he carried with him."

"Was it Quadling? My word! What a terrible Nemesis. Well, *nil nisi bonum*, but I never thought much of the chap, and your friend the Countess has had an escape. But now, sir, I must be moving. My engagement is for twelve noon. If you want me, mind you send—207 Rue Miromesnil, or to the Embassy; but let us arrange to meet this evening, eh? Dinner and a theatre—what do you say?"

Then Colonel Papillon rode off, and the General was driven to the Boulevard des Capucines, having much to occupy his thoughts by the way.

It did not greatly please him to have this story of the Countess's relations with Quadling, as first hinted at by the police, endorsed now by his friend Papillon. Clearly she had kept up her acquaintance, her intimacy to the very last: why otherwise should she have received him, alone, been closeted with him for an hour or more on the very eve of his flight? It was a clandestine acquaintance

too, or seemed so, for Sir Charles, although a frequent
visitor at her house, had never met Quadling there.

What did it all mean? And yet, what, after all, did it
matter to him?

A good deal really more than he chose to admit to
himself, even now, when closely questioning his secret
heart. The fact was, the Countess had made a very strong
impression on him from the first. He had admired her
greatly during the past winter at Rome, but then it was
only a passing fancy, as he thought,–the pleasant platonic
flirtation of a middle-aged man, who never expected to
inspire or feel a great love. Only now, when he had
shared a serious trouble with her, had passed through
common difficulties and dangers, he was finding what
accident may do–how it may fan a first liking into a
stronger flame. It was absurd, of course. He was fifty-one,
he had weathered many trifling affairs of the heart, and
here he was, bowled over at last, and by a woman he was
not certain was entitled to his respect.

What was he to do?

The answer came at once and unhesitatingly, as it
would to any other honest, chivalrous gentleman.

"By George, I'll stick to her through thick and thin! I'll
trust her whatever happens or has happened, come what
may. Such a woman as that is above suspicion. She *must*
be straight. I should be a beast and a blackguard double
distilled to think anything else. I am sure she can put all
right with a word, can explain everything when she
chooses. I will wait till she does."

Thus fortified and decided, Sir Charles took his way to
the Hôtel Madagascar about noon. At the desk he
inquired for the Countess, and begged that his card might
be sent up to her. The man looked at it, then at the
visitor, as he stood there waiting rather impatiently, then
again at the card. At last he walked out and across the
inner courtyard of the hotel to the office. Presently the

manager came back, bowing low, and, holding the card in his hand, began a desultory conversation.

"Yes, yes," cried the General, angrily cutting short all references to the weather and the number of English visitors in Paris. "But be so good as to let Madame la Comtesse know that I have called."

"Ah, to be sure! I came to tell Monsieur le Général that madame will hardly be able to see him. She is indisposed, I believe. At any rate, she does not receive to-day."

"As to that, we shall see. I will take no answer except direct from her. Take or send up my card without further delay. I insist! Do you hear?" said the General, so fiercely that the manager turned tail and fled up-stairs.

Perhaps he yielded his ground the more readily that he saw over the General's shoulder the figure of Galipaud the detective looming in the archway. It had been arranged that, as it was not advisable to have the inspector hanging about the courtyard of the hotel, the clerk or the manager should keep watch over the Countess and detain any visitors who might call upon her. Galipaud had taken post at a wine-shop over the way, and was to be summoned whenever his presence was thought necessary.

There he was now, standing just behind the General, and for the present unseen by him.

But then a telegraph messenger came in and up to the desk. He held the usual blue envelope in his hand, and called out the name on the address:

"Castagneto. Contessa Castagneto."

At sound of which the General turned sharply, to find Galipaud advancing and stretching out his hand to take the message.

"Pardon me," cried Sir Charles, promptly interposing and understanding the situation at a glance. "I am just going up to see that lady. Give me the telegram."

Galipaud would have disputed the point, when the General, who had already recognized him, said quietly:

"No, no, Inspector, you have no earthly right to it. I guess why you are here, but you are not entitled to interfere with private correspondence. Stand back;" and seeing the detective hesitate, he added peremptorily:

"Enough of this. I order you to get out of the way. And be quick about it!"

The manager now returned, and admitted that Madame la Comtesse would receive her visitor. A few seconds more, and the General was admitted into her presence.

"How truly kind of you to call!" she said at once, coming up to him with both hands outstretched and frank gladness in her eyes.

Yes, she was very attractive in her plain, dark travelling dress draping her tall, graceful figure; her beautiful, pale face was enhanced by the rich tones of her dark brown, wavy hair, while just a narrow band of white muslin at her wrists and neck set off the dazzling clearness of her skin.

"Of course I came. I thought you might want me, or might like to know the latest news," he answered, as he held her hands in his for a few seconds longer than was perhaps absolutely necessary.

"Oh, do tell me! Is there anything fresh?" There was a flash of crimson colour in her cheek, which faded almost instantly. "This much. They have found out who the man was."

"Really? Positively? Whom do they say now?"

"Perhaps I had better not tell you. It may surprise you, shock you to hear. I think you knew him–"

"Nothing can well shock me now. I have had too many shocks already. Who do they think it is?"

"A Mr. Quadling, a banker, who is supposed to have absconded from Rome."

She received the news so impassively, with such strange self-possession, that for a moment he was disappointed in her. But then, quick to excuse, he suggested:

"You may have already heard?"

"Yes; the police people at the railway station told me they thought it was Mr. Quadling."

"But you knew him?"

"Certainly. They were my bankers, much to my sorrow. I shall lose heavily by their failure."

"That also has reached you, then?" interrupted the General, hastily and somewhat uneasily.

"To be sure. The man told me of it himself. Indeed, he came to me the very day I was leaving Rome, and made me an offer—a most obliging offer."

"To share his fallen fortunes?"

"Sir Charles Collingham! How can you? That creature!" The contempt in her tone was immeasurable.

"I had heard—well, someone said that—"

"Speak out, General; I shall not be offended. I know what you mean. It is perfectly true that the man once presumed to pester me with his attentions. But I would as soon have looked at a courier or a cook. And now—"

There was a pause. The General felt on delicate ground. He could ask no questions—anything more must come from the Countess herself.

"But let me tell you what his offer was. I don't know why I listened to it. I ought to have at once informed the police. I wish I had."

"It might have saved him from his fate."

"Every villain gets his deserts in the long run," she said, with bitter sententiousness. "And this Mr. Quadling is—But wait, you shall know him better. He came to me to propose—what do you think?—that he—his bank, I mean—should secretly repay me the amount of my deposit, all the money I had in it. To join me in his fraud, in fact—"

"The scoundrel! Upon my word, he has been well served. And that was the last you saw of him?"

"I saw him on the journey, at Turin, at Modane, at—Oh, Sir Charles, do not ask me any more about him!" she cried, with a sudden outburst, half-grief, half-dread. "I cannot tell you–I am obliged to–I–I–"

"Then do not say another word," he said, promptly.

"There are other things. But my lips are sealed–at least for the present. You do not–will not think any worse of me?"

She laid her hand gently on his arm, and his closed over it with such evident good-will that a blush crimsoned her cheek. It still hung there, and deepened when he said, warmly:

"As if anything could make me do that! Don't you know–you may not, but let me assure you, Countess–that nothing could happen to shake me in the high opinion I have of you. Come what may, I shall trust you, believe in you, think well of you–always."

"How sweet of you to say that! and now, of all times," she murmured quite softly, and looking up for the first time, shyly, to meet his eyes.

Her hand was still on his arm, covered by his, and she nestled so close to him that it was easy, natural, indeed, for him to slip his other arm around her waist and draw her to him.

"And now–of all times–may I say one word more?" he whispered in her ear. "Will you give me the right to shelter and protect you, to stand by you, share your troubles, or keep them from you–?"

"No, no, no, indeed, not now!" She looked up appealingly, the tears brimming up in her bright eyes. "I cannot, will not accept this sacrifice. You are only speaking out of your true-hearted chivalry. You must not join yourself to me, you must not involve yourself–"

He stopped her protests by the oldest and most effectual method known in such cases. That first sweet kiss sealed the compact so quickly entered into between them.

And after that she surrendered at discretion. There was no more hesitation or reluctance; she accepted his love as he had offered it, freely, with whole heart and soul, crept up under his sheltering wing like a storm-beaten dove reentering the nest, and there, cooing softly, "My knight—my own true knight and lord," yielded herself willingly and unquestioningly to his tender caresses.

Such moments snatched from the heart of pressing anxieties are made doubly sweet by their sharp contrast with a background of trouble.

16

They sat there, these two, hand locked in hand, saying little, satisfied now to be with each other and their new-found love. The time flew by far too fast, till at last Sir Charles, with a half-laugh, suggested:

"Do you know, dearest Countess—"

She corrected him in a soft, low voice.

"My name is Sabine—Charles."

"Sabine, darling. It is very prosaic of me, perhaps, but do you know that I am nearly starved? I came on here at once. I have had no breakfast."

"Nor have I," she answered, smiling. "I was thinking of it when—when you appeared like a whirlwind, and since then, events have moved so fast."

"Are you sorry, Sabine? Would you rather go back to—to—before?" She made a pretty gesture of closing his traitor lips with her small hand.

"Not for worlds. But you soldiers—you are terrible men! Who can resist you?"

"Bah! It is you who are irresistible. But there, why not put on your jacket and let us go out to lunch somewhere—Durand's, Voisin's, the Café de le Paix? Which do you prefer?"

"I suppose they will not try to stop us?"

"Who should try?" he asked.

"The people of the hotel—the police—I cannot exactly say whom; but I dread something of the sort. I don't quite understand that manager. He has been up to see me several times, and he spoke rather oddly, rather rudely."

"Then he shall answer for it," snorted Sir Charles, hotly. "It is the fault of that brute of a detective, I suppose. Still they would hardly dare—"

"A detective? What? Here? Are you sure?"

"Perfectly sure. It is one of those from the Lyons Station. I knew him again directly, and he was inclined to be interfering. Why, I caught him trying–but that reminds me–I rescued this telegram from his clutches."

He took the little blue envelope from his breast pocket and handed it to her, kissing the tips of her fingers as she took it from him.

"Ah!"

A sudden ejaculation of dismay escaped her, when, after rather carelessly tearing the message open, she had glanced at it.

"What is the matter?" he asked in eager solicitude. "May I not know?"

She made no offer to give him the telegram, and said in a faltering voice, and with much hesitation of manner, "I do not know. I hardly think–of course I do not like to withhold anything, not now. And yet, this is a business which concerns me only, I am afraid. I ought not to drag you into it."

"What concerns you is very much my business, too. I do not wish to force your confidence, still–"

She gave him the telegram quite obediently, with a little sigh of relief, glad to realize now, for the first time after many years, that there was someone to give her orders and take the burden of trouble off her shoulders.

He read it, but did not understand it in the least. It ran: "I must see you immediately, and beg you will come. You will find Hortense here. She is giving trouble. You only can deal with her. Do not delay. Come at once, or we must go to you.–Ripaldi, Hôtel Ivoire, Rue Bellechasse."

"What does this mean? Who sends it? Who is Ripaldi?" asked Sir Charles, rather brusquely.

"He–he–oh, Charles, I shall have to go. Anything would be better than his coming here."

"Ripaldi? Haven't I heard the name? He was one of those in the sleeping-car, I think? The Chief of the Detective Police called it out once or twice. Am I not right? Please tell me–am I not right?"

"Yes, yes; this man was there with the rest of us. A dark man, who sat near the door—"

"Ah, to be sure. But what—what in Heaven's name has he to do with you? How does he dare to send you such an impudent message as this? Surely, Sabine, you will tell me? You will admit that I have a right to ask?"

"Yes, of course. I will tell you, Charles, everything; but not here—not now. It must be on the way. I have been very wrong, very foolish—but oh, come, come, do let us be going. I am so afraid he might—"

"Then I may go with you? You do not object to that?"

"I much prefer it—much. Do let us make haste!"

She snatched up her sealskin jacket, and held it to him prettily, that he might help her into it, which he did neatly and cleverly, smoothing her great puffed-out sleeves under each shoulder of the coat, still talking eagerly and taking no toll for his trouble as she stood patiently, passively before him.

"And this Hortense? It is your maid, is it not—the woman who had taken herself off? How comes it that she is with that Italian fellow? Upon my soul, I don't understand—not a little bit."

"I cannot explain that, either. It is most strange, most incomprehensible, but we shall soon know. Please, Charles, please do not get impatient."

They passed together down into the hotel courtyard and across it, under the archway which led past the clerk's desk into the street.

On seeing them, he came out hastily and placed himself in front, quite plainly barring their egress.

"Oh, madame, one moment," he said in a tone that was by no means conciliatory. "The manager wants to speak to you; he told me to tell you, and stop you if you went out."

"The manager can speak to madame when she returns," interposed the General angrily, answering for the Countess.

"I have had my orders, and I cannot allow her—"

"Stand aside, you scoundrel!" cried the General, blazing up; "or upon my soul I shall give you such a lesson you will be sorry you were ever born."

At this moment the manager himself appeared in reinforcement, and the clerk turned to him for protection and support.

"I was merely giving madame your message, M. Auguste, when this gentleman interposed, threatened me, maltreated me—"

"Oh, surely not; it is some mistake;" the manager spoke most suavely. "But certainly I did wish to speak to madame. I wished to ask her whether she was satisfied with her apartment. I find that the rooms she has generally occupied have fallen vacant, in the nick of time. Perhaps madame would like to look at them, and move?"

"Thank you, M. Auguste, you are very good; but at another time. I am very much pressed just now. When I return in an hour or two, not now."

The manager was profuse in his apologies, and made no further difficulty.

"Oh, as you please, madame. Perfectly. By and by, later, when you choose."

The fact was, the desired result had been obtained. For now, on the far side from where he had been watching, Galipaud appeared, no doubt in reply to some secret signal, and the detective with a short nod in acknowledgment had evidently removed his embargo.

A cab was called, and Sir Charles, having put the Countess in, was turning to give the driver his instructions, when a fresh complication arose.

Someone coming round the corner had caught a glimpse of the lady disappearing into the fiacre, and cried out from afar.

"Stay! Stop! I want to speak to that lady; detain her." It was the sharp voice of little M. Floçon, whom most of those present, certainly the Countess and Sir Charles, immediately recognized.

"No, no, no—don't let them keep me—I cannot wait now," she whispered in earnest, urgent appeal. It was not lost on her loyal and devoted friend.

"Go on!" he shouted to the cabman, with all the peremptory insistence of one trained to give words of command. "Forward! As fast as you can drive. I'll pay you double fare. Tell him where to go, Sabine. I'll follow—in less than no time."

The fiacre rattled off at top speed, and the General turned to confront M. Floçon.

The little detective was white to the lips with rage and disappointment; but he also was a man of promptitude, and before falling foul of this pestilent Englishman, who had again marred his plans, he shouted to Galipaud—

"Quick! After them! Follow her wherever she goes. Take this,"—he thrust a paper into his subordinate's hand. "It is a warrant for her arrest. Seize her wherever you find her, and bring her to the Quai l'Horloge," the euphemistic title of the headquarters of the French police.

The pursuit was started at once, and then the Chief turned upon Sir Charles. "Now it is between us," he said, fiercely. "You must account to me for what you have done."

"Must I?" answered the General, mockingly and with a little laugh.

"It is perfectly easy. Madame was in a hurry, so I helped her to get away. That was all."

"You have traversed and opposed the action of the law. You have impeded me, the Chief of the Detective Service, in the execution of my duty. It is not the first time, but now you must answer for it."

"Dear me!" said the General in the same flippant, irritating tone.

"You will have to accompany me now to the Prefecture."

"And if it does not suit me to go?"

"I will have you carried there, bound, tied hand and foot, by the police, like any common rapscallion taken in the act who resists the authority of an officer."

"Oho, you talk very big, sir. Perhaps you will be so obliging as to tell me what I have done."

"You have connived at the escape of a criminal from justice—"

"That lady? Psha!"

"She is charged with a heinous crime—that in which you yourself were implicated—the murder of that man on the train."

"Bah! You must be a stupid goose, to hint at such a thing! A lady of birth, breeding, the highest respectability—impossible!"

"All that has not prevented her from allying herself with base, common wretches. I do not say she struck the blow, but I believe she inspired, concerted, approved it, leaving her confederates to do the actual deed."

"Confederates?"

"The man Ripaldi, your Italian fellow traveller; her maid, Hortense Petitpré, who was missing this morning."

The General was fairly staggered at this unexpected blow. Half an hour ago he would have scouted the very thought, indignantly repelled the spoken words that even hinted a suspicion of Sabine Castagneto. But that telegram, signed Ripaldi, the introduction of the maid's name, and the suggestion that she was troublesome, the threat that if the Countess did not go, they would come to her, and her marked uneasiness thereat—all this implied plainly the existence of collusion, of some secret relations, some secret understanding between her and the others.

He could not entirely conceal the trouble that now overcame him; it certainly did not escape so shrewd an observer as M. Floçon, who promptly tried to turn it to good account.

"Come, M. le Général," he said, with much assumed *bonhomie.* "I can see how it is with you, and you have my sincere sympathy. We are all of us liable to be carried away, and there is much excuse for you in this. But now—believe me, I am justified in saying it —now I tell you that our case is strong against her, that it is not mere speculation, but supported by facts. Now surely you will come over to our side?"

"In what way?"

"Tell us frankly all you know—where that lady has gone, help us to lay our hands on her."

"Your own people will do that. I heard you order that man to follow her."

"Probably; still I would rather have the information from you. It would satisfy me of your good-will. I need not then proceed to extremities—"

"I certainly shall not give it you," said the General, hotly. "Anything I know about or have heard from the Contessa Castagneto is sacred; besides, I still believe in her—thoroughly. Nothing you have said can shake me."

"Then I must ask you to accompany me to the Prefecture. You will come, I trust, on my invitation." The Chief spoke quietly, but with considerable dignity, and he laid a slight stress upon the last word.

"Meaning that if I do not, you will have resort to something stronger?"

"That will be quite unnecessary, I am sure,—at least I hope so. Still—"

"I will go where you like, only I will tell you nothing more, not a single word; and before I start, I must let my friends at the Embassy know where to find me."

"Oh, with all my heart," said the little detective, shrugging his shoulders. "We will call there on our way, and you can tell the porter. They will know where to find us."

17

Sir Charles Collingham and his escort, M. Floçon, entered a cab together and were driven first to the Faubourg St. Honoré. The General tried hard to maintain his nonchalance, but he was yet a little crestfallen at the turn things had taken, and M. Floçon, who, on the other hand, was elated and triumphant, saw it. But no words passed between them until they arrived at the portals of the British Embassy, and the General handed out his card to the magnificent porter who received them.

"Kindly let Colonel Papillon have that without delay." The General had written a few words: "I have got into fresh trouble. Come on to me at the Police Prefecture if you can spare the time."

"The Colonel is now in the Chancery: will not monsieur wait?" asked the porter, with superb civility.

But the detective would not suffer this, and interposed, answering abruptly for Sir Charles:

"No. It is impossible. We are going to the Quai l'Horloge. It is an urgent matter."

The porter knew what the Quai l'Horloge meant, and he guessed intuitively who was speaking. Every Frenchman can recognize a police officer, and has, as a rule, no great opinion of him. "Very well!" now said the porter, curtly, as he banged the wicket-gate on the retreating cab, and he did not hurry himself in giving the card to Colonel Papillon.

"Does this mean that I am a prisoner?" asked Sir Charles, his gorge rising, as it did easily.

"It means, monsieur, that you are in the hands of justice until your recent conduct has been fully explained," said the detective, with the air of a despot.

"But I protest—"

"I wish to hear no further observations, monsieur. You may reserve them till you can give them to the right person."

The General's temper was sorely ruffled. He did not like it at all; yet what could he do? Prudence gained the day, and after a struggle he decided to submit, lest worse might befall him.

There was, in truth, worse to be encountered. It was very irksome to be in the power of this now domineering little man on his own ground, and eager to show his power. It was with a very bad grace that Sir Charles obeyed the curt orders he received, to leave the cab, to enter at a side door of the Prefecture, to follow this pompous conductor along the long vaulted passages of this rambling building, up many flights of stone stairs, to halt obediently at his command when at length they reached a closed door on an upper story.

"It is here!" said M. Floçon, as he turned the handle unceremoniously without knocking. "Enter."

A man was seated at a small desk in the centre of a big bare room, who rose at once at the sight of M. Floçon, and bowed deferentially without speaking.

"Baume," said the Chief, shortly, "I wish to leave this gentleman with you. Make him at home,"–the words were spoken in manifest irony,–"and when I call you, bring him at once to my cabinet. You, monsieur, you will oblige me by staying here."

Sir Charles nodded carelessly, took the first chair that offered, and sat down by the fire.

He was to all intents and purposes in custody, and he examined his gaoler at first wrathfully, then curiously, struck with his rather strange figure and appearance. Baume, as the Chief had called him, was a short, thick-set man with a great shock head sunk in low between a pair of enormous shoulders, betokening great physical strength; he stood on very thin but greatly twisted bow legs, and the quaintness of his figure was emphasized by the short black blouse or smock-frock he wore over his other clothes like a French artisan.

He was a man of few words, and those not the most polite in tone, for when the General began with a banal remark about the weather, M. Baume replied, shortly:

"I wish to have no talk;" and when Sir Charles pulled out his cigarette-case, as he did almost automatically from time to time when in any situation of annoyance or perplexity, Baume raised his hand warningly and grunted:

"Not allowed."

"Then I'll be hanged if I don't smoke in spite of every man jack of you!" cried the General, hotly, rising from his seat and speaking unconsciously in English.

"What's that?" asked Baume, gruffly. He was one of the detective staff, and was only doing his duty according to his lights, and he said so with such an injured air that the General was pacified, laughed, and relapsed into silence without lighting his cigarette.

The time ran on, from minutes into nearly an hour, a very trying wait for Sir Charles. There is always something irritating in doing antechamber work, in kicking one's heels in the waiting-room of any functionary or official, high or low, and the General found it hard to possess himself in patience, when he thought he was being thus ignominiously treated by a man like M. Floçon. All the time, too, he was worrying himself about the Countess, wondering first how she had fared; next, where she was just then; last of all, and longest, whether it was possible for her to be mixed up in anything compromising or criminal.

Suddenly an electric bell struck in the room. There was a table telephone at Baume's elbow; he took up the handle, put the tube to his mouth and ear, got his message answered, and then, rising, said abruptly to Sir Charles:

"Come."

When the General was at last ushered into the presence of the Chief of the Detective Police, he found to his satisfaction that Colonel Papillon was also there, and at M. Floçon's side sat the instructing judge, M. Beaumont le Hardi, who, after waiting politely until the two Englishmen had exchanged greetings, was the first to speak, and in apology.

"You will, I trust, pardon us, M. le Général, for having detained you here and so long. But there were, as we thought, good and sufficient reasons. If those have now lost some of their cogency, we still stand by our action as having been justifiable in the execution of our duty. We are now willing to let you go free, because–because–"

"We have caught the person, the lady you helped to escape," blurted out the detective, unable to resist making the point.

"The Countess? Is she here, in custody? Never!"

"Undoubtedly she is in custody, and in very close custody too," went on M. Floçon, gleefully. " *Au secret*, if you know what that means–in a cell separate and apart, where no one is permitted to see or speak to her."

"Surely not that? Jack–Papillon–this must not be. I beg of you, implore, insist, that you will get his lordship to interpose."

"But, sir, how can I? You must not ask impossibilities. The Contessa Castagneto is really an Italian subject now."

"She is English by birth, and whether or no, she is a woman, a high-bred lady; and it is abominable, unheard-of, to subject her to such monstrous treatment," said the General.

"But these gentlemen declare that they are fully warranted, that she has put herself in the wrong–greatly, culpably in the wrong."

"I don't believe it!" cried the General, indignantly. "Not from these chaps, a pack of idiots, always on the wrong tack! I don't believe a word, not if they swear."

"But they have documentary evidence–papers of the most damaging kind against her."

"Where? How?"

"He–M. le Juge–has been showing me a note-book;" and the General's eyes, following Jack Papillon's, were directed to a small *carnet*, or memorandum-book, which the Judge, interpreting the glance, was tapping significantly with his finger.

Then the Judge said blandly, "It is easy to perceive that you protest, M. le Général, against that lady's arrest. Is it so? Well, we are not called upon to justify it to you, not in the very least. But we are dealing with a brave man, a gentleman, an officer of high rank and consideration, and you shall know things that we are not bound to tell, to you or to any one."

"First," he continued, holding up the note-book, "do you know what this is? Have you ever seen it before?"

"I am dimly conscious of the fact, and yet I cannot say when or where."

"It is the property of one of your fellow travellers–an Italian called Ripaldi."

"Ripaldi?" said the General, remembering with some uneasiness that he had seen the name at the bottom of the Countess's telegram. "Ah! now I understand."

"You had heard of it, then? In what connection?" asked the Judge, a little carelessly, but it was a suddenly planned pitfall.

"I now understand," replied the General, perfectly on his guard, "why the note-book was familiar to me. I had seen it in that man's hands in the waiting-room. He was writing in it."

"Indeed? A favourite occupation evidently. He was fond of confiding in that note-book, and committed to it much that he never expected would see the light–his movements, intentions, ideas, even his inmost thoughts. The book–which he no doubt lost inadvertently is very incriminating to himself and his friends."

"What do you imply?" hastily inquired Sir Charles.

"Simply that it is on that which is written here that we base one part, perhaps the strongest, of our case against the Countess. It is strangely but convincingly corroborative of our suspicions against her."

"May I look at it for myself?" went on the General in a tone of contemptuous disbelief.

"It is in Italian. Perhaps you can read that language? If not, I have translated the most important passages," said the Judge, offering some other papers.

"Thank you; if you will permit me, I should prefer to look at the original;" and the General, without more ado, stretched out his hand and took the note-book.

What he read there, as he quickly scanned its pages, shall be told in the next chapter. It will be seen that there were things written that looked very damaging to his dear friend, Sabine Castagneto.

18

Ripaldi's diary–its ownership plainly shown by the record of his name in full, Natale Ripaldi, inside the cover–was a commonplace note-book bound in shabby drab cloth, its edges and corners strengthened with some sort of white metal. The pages were of coarse paper, lined blue and red, and they were dog-eared and smirched as though they had been constantly turned over and used.

The earlier entries were little more than a record of work to do or done.

"Jan. 11. To call at Café di Roma, 12.30. Beppo will meet me.

"Jan. 13. Traced M. L. Last employed as a model at S.'s studio, Palazzo B.

"Jan. 15. There is trouble brewing at the Circulo Bonafede; Louvaih, Malatesta, and the Englishman Sprot, have joined it. All are noted Anarchists.

"Jan. 20. Mem., pay Trattore. The Bestia will not wait. X. is also pressing, and Mariuccia. Situation tightens.

"Jan. 23. Ordered to watch Q. Could I work him? No. Strong doubts of his solvency.

"Feb. 10, 11, 12. After Q. No grounds yet.

"Feb. 27. Q. keeps up good appearance. Any mistake? Shall I try him? Sorely pressed. X. threatens me with Prefettura.

"March 1. Q. in difficulties. Out late every night. Is playing high; poor luck.

"March 3. Q. means mischief. Preparing for a start?

"March 10. Saw Q. about, here, there, everywhere."

Then followed a brief account of Quadling's movements on the day before his departure from Rome, very much as they have been described in a previous chapter. These were made mostly in the form of reflections, conjectures, hopes, and fears; hurry-scurry of pursuit had no doubt broken the immediate record of events, and these had been entered next day in the train.

"March 17 (the day previous). He has not shown up. I thought to see him at the buffet at Genoa. The conductor took him his coffee to the car. I hoped to have begun an acquaintance.

"12.30. Breakfasted at Turin. Q. did not come to table. Found him hanging about outside restaurant. Spoke; got short reply. Wishes to avoid observation, I suppose.

"But he speaks to others. He has claimed acquaintance with madame's lady's maid, and he wants to speak to the mistress. 'Tell her I must speak to her,' I heard him say, as I passed close to them. Then they separated hurriedly. "At Modane he came to the Douane, and afterwards into the restaurant. He bowed across the table to the lady. She hardly recognized him, which is odd. Of course she must know him; then why–? There is something between them, and the maid is in it.

"What shall *I* do? I could spoil any game of theirs if I stepped in. What are they after? His money, no doubt.

"So am I; I have the best right to it, for I can do most for him. He is absolutely in my power, and he'll see that– he's no fool– directly he knows who I am, and why I'm here. It will be worth his while to buy me off, if I'm ready to sell myself, and my duty, and the Prefettura–and why shouldn't I? What better can I do? Shall I ever have such a chance again? Twenty, thirty, forty thousand lire, more, even, at one stroke; why, it's a fortune! I could go to the Republic, to America, North or South, send for Mariuccia– no, *cos petto*! I will continue free! I will spend the money on myself, as I alone will have earned it, and at such risk.

"I have worked it out thus:

"I will go to him at the very last, just before we are reaching Paris. Tell him, threaten him with arrest, then give him his chance of escape. No fear that he won't accept it; he *must*, whatever he may have settled with the others. *Altro!* I snap my fingers at them. He has most to fear from me."

The next entries were made after some interval, a long interval, –no doubt, after the terrible deed had been done,–and the words were traced with trembling fingers, so that the writing was most irregular and scarcely legible.

"Ugh! I am still trembling with horror and fear. I cannot get it out of my mind; I never shall. Why, what tempted me? How could I bring myself to do it?

"But for these two women–they are fiends, furies–it would never have been necessary. Now one of them has escaped, and the other– she is here, so cold-blooded, so self-possessed and quiet–who would have thought it of her? That she, a lady of rank and high breeding, gentle, delicate, tender-hearted. Tender? the fiend! Oh, shall I ever forget her?

"And now she has me in her power! But have I not her also? We are in the same boat–we must sink or swim, together. We are equally bound, I to her, she to me. What are we to do? How shall we meet inquiry? *Santissima Donna!* why did I not risk it, and climb out like the maid? It was terrible for the moment, but the worst would have been over, and now–"

There was yet more, scribbled in the same faltering, agitated handwriting, and from the context the entries had been made in the waiting-room of the railroad station.

"I must attract her attention. She will not look my way. I want her to understand that I have something special to say to her, and that, as we are forbidden to speak, I am writing it herein–that she must contrive to take the book from me and read unobserved.

" *Cos petto!* she is stupid! Has fear dazed her entirely? No matter, I will set it all down."

Now followed what the police deemed such damaging evidence.

"Countess. Remember. Silence–absolute silence. Not a word as to who I am, or what is common knowledge to us both. It is done. That cannot be undone. Be brave, resolute; admit nothing. Stick to it that you know nothing, heard nothing. Deny that you knew *him*, or me. Swear you slept soundly the night through, make some excuse, say you were drugged, anything, only be on your guard, and say nothing about me. I warn you. Leave me alone. Or–but your interests are my interests; we must stand or fall together. Afterwards I will meet you–I *must* meet you somewhere. If we miss at the station front, write to me Poste Restante, Grand Hôtel, and give me an address. This is imperative. Once more, silence and discretion."

This ended the writing in the note-book, and the whole perusal occupied Sir Charles from fifteen to twenty minutes, during which the French officials watched his face closely, and his friend Colonel Papillon anxiously.

But the General's mask was impenetrable, and at the end of his reading he turned back to read and re-read many pages, holding the book to the light, and seeming to examine the contents very curiously.

"Well?" said the Judge at last, when he met the General's eye.

"Do you lay great store by this evidence?" asked the General in a calm, dispassionate voice.

"Is it not natural that we should? Is it not strongly, conclusively incriminating?"

"It would be so, of course, if it were to be depended upon. But as to that I have my doubts, and grave doubts."

"Bah!" interposed the detective; "that is mere conjecture, mere assertion. Why should not the book be believed? It is perfectly genuine–"

"Wait, sir," said the General, raising his hand. "Have you not noticed–surely it cannot have escaped so astute a police functionary—that the entries are not all in the same handwriting?"

"What! Oh, that is too absurd!" cried both the officials in a breath.

They saw at once that if this discovery were admitted to be an absolute fact, the whole drift of their conclusions must be changed.

"Examine the book for yourselves. To my mind it is perfectly clear and beyond all question," insisted Sir Charles. "I am quite positive that the last pages were written by a different hand from the first."

19

For several minutes both the Judge and the detective pored over the note-book, examining page after page, shaking their heads, and declining to accept the evidence of their eyes.

"I cannot see it," said the Judge at last; adding reluctantly, "No doubt there is a difference, but it is to be explained."

"Quite so," put in M. Floçon. "When he wrote the early part, he was calm and collected; the last entries, so straggling, so ragged, and so badly written, were made when he was fresh from the crime, excited, upset, little master of himself. Naturally he would use a different hand."

"Or he would wish to disguise it. It was likely he would so wish," further remarked the Judge.

"You admit, then, that there is a difference?" argued the General, shrewdly. "But there is more than a disguise. The best disguise leaves certain unchangeable features. Some letters, capital G's, H's, and others, will betray themselves through the best disguise. I know what I am saying. I have studied the subject of handwriting; it interests me. These are the work of two different hands. Call in an expert; you will find I am right."

"Well, well," said the Judge, after a pause, "let us grant your position for the moment. What do you deduce? What do you infer therefrom?"

"Surely you can see what follows—what this leads us to?" said Sir Charles, rather disdainfully.

"I have formed an opinion—yes, but I should like to see if it coincides with yours. You think—"

"I know," corrected the General. "I know that, as two persons wrote in that book, either it is not Ripaldi's book, or the last of them was not Ripaldi. I saw the last writer at his work, saw him with my own eyes. Yet he did not write with Ripaldi's hand– this is incontestable, I am sure of it, I will swear it–ergo, he is not Ripaldi."

"But you should have known this at the time," interjected M. Floçon, fiercely. "Why did you not discover the change of identity? You should have seen that this was not Ripaldi."

"Pardon me. I did not know the man. I had not noticed him particularly on the journey. There was no reason why I should. I had no communication, no dealings, with any of my fellow passengers except my brother and the Countess."

"But some of the others would surely have remarked the change?" went on the Judge, greatly puzzled. "That alone seems enough to condemn your theory, M. le General."

"I take my stand on fact, not theory," stoutly maintained Sir Charles, "and I am satisfied I am right."

"But if that was not Ripaldi, who was it? Who would wish to masquerade in his dress and character, to make entries of that sort, as if under his hand?"

"Someone determined to divert suspicion from himself to others–"

"But stay–does he not plainly confess his own guilt?"

"What matter if he is not Ripaldi? Directly the inquiry was over, he could steal away and resume his own personality–that of a man supposed to be dead, and therefore safe from all interference and future pursuit."

"You mean–Upon my word, I compliment you, M. le Général. It is really ingenious! Remarkable, indeed! Superb!" cried the Judge, and only professional jealousy prevented M. Floçon from conceding the same praise.

"But how–what–I do not understand," asked Colonel Papillon in amazement. His wits did not travel quite so fast as those of his companions.

"Simply this, my dear Jack," explained the General: "Ripaldi must have tried to blackmail Quadling, as he proposed, and Quadling turned the tables on him. They fought, no doubt, and Quadling killed him, possibly in self-defence. He would have said so, but in his peculiar position as an absconding defaulter he did not dare. That is how I read it, and I believe that now these gentlemen are disposed to agree with me."

"In theory, certainly," said the Judge, heartily. "But oh! for some more positive proof of this change of character! If we could only identify the corpse, prove clearly that it is not Quadling. And still more, if we had not let this so-called Ripaldi slip through our fingers! You will never find him, M. Floçon, never."

The detective hung his head in guilty admission of this reproach.

"We may help you in both these difficulties, gentlemen," said Sir Charles, pleasantly. "My friend here, Colonel Papillon, can speak as to the man Quadling. He knew him well in Rome, a year or two ago."

"Please wait one moment only;" the detective touched a bell, and briefly ordered two fiacres to the door at once.

"That is right, M. Floçon," said the Judge. "We will all go to the Morgue. The body is there by now. You will not refuse your assistance, monsieur?"

"One moment. As to the other matter, M. le General?" went on M. Floçon. "Can you help us to find this miscreant, whoever he may be?"

"Yes. The man who calls himself Ripaldi is to be found—or, at least, you would have found him an hour or so ago—at the Hotel Ivoire, Rue Bellechasse. But time has been lost, I fear."

"Nevertheless, we will send there."

"The woman Hortense was also with him when last I heard of them."

"How do you know?" began the detective, suspiciously.

"Psha!" interrupted the Judge; "that will keep. This is the time for action, and we owe too much to the General to distrust him now."

"Thank you; I am pleased to hear you say that," went on Sir Charles. "But if I have been of some service to you, perhaps you owe me a little in return. That poor lady! Think what she is suffering. Surely, to oblige me, you will now set her free?"

"Indeed, monsieur, I fear–I do not see how, consistently with my duty"–protested the Judge.

"At least allow her to return to her hotel. She can remain there at your disposal. I will promise you that."

"How can you answer for her?"

"She will do what I ask, I think, if I may send her just two or three lines."

The Judge yielded, smiling at the General's urgency, and shrewdly guessing what it implied.

Then the three departures from the Prefecture took place within a short time of each other.

A posse of police went to arrest Ripaldi; the Countess returned to the Hotel Madagascar; and the Judge's party started for the Morgue,–only a short journey,–where they were presently received with every mark of respect and consideration.

The keeper, or officer in charge, was summoned, and came out bareheaded to the fiacre, bowing low before his distinguished visitors.

"Good morning, La Pêche," said M. Floçon in a sharp voice. "We have come for an identification. The body from the Lyons Station –he of the murder in the sleeping-car– is it yet arrived?"

"But surely, at your service, Chief," replied the old man, obsequiously. "If the gentlemen will give themselves the trouble to enter the office, I will lead them behind, direct into the mortuary chamber. There are many people in yonder."

It was the usual crowd of sightseers passing slowly before the plate glass of this, the most terrible shop-front in the world, where the goods exposed, the merchandise, are hideous corpses laid out in rows upon the marble slabs, the battered, tattered remnants of outraged humanity, insulted by the most terrible indignities in death.

Who make up this curious throng, and what strange morbid motives drag them there? Those fat, comfortable-looking women, with their baskets on their arms; the decent workmen in dusty blouses, idling between the hours of work; the riffraff of the streets, male or female, in various stages of wretchedness and degradation? A few, no doubt, are impelled by motives we cannot challenge—they are torn and tortured by suspense, trembling lest they may recognize missing dear ones among the exposed; others stare carelessly at the day's "take," wondering, perhaps, if they may come to the same fate; one or two are idle sightseers, not always French, for the Morgue is a favourite haunt with the irrepressible tourist doing Paris. Strangest of all, the murderer himself, the doer of the fell deed, comes here, to the very spot where his victim lies stark and reproachful, and stares at it spellbound, fascinated, filled more with remorse, perchance, than fear at the risk he runs. So common is this trait, that in mysterious murder cases the police of Paris keep a disguised officer among the crowd at the Morgue, and have thereby made many memorable arrests.

"This way, gentlemen, this way;" and the keeper of the Morgue led the party through one or two rooms into the inner and back recesses of the buildings. It was behind the scenes of the Morgue, and they were made free of its most gruesome secrets as they passed along.

The temperature had suddenly fallen far below freezing-point, and the icy cold chilled to the very marrow. Still worse was an all-pervading, acrid odour of artificially suspended animal decay. The cold-air process, that latest of scientific contrivances to arrest the waste of tissue, has now been applied at the Morgue to preserve and keep the bodies fresh, and allow them to be for a longer time exposed than when running water was the only aid. There are, moreover, many specially contrived refrigerating chests, in which those still unrecognized corpses are laid by for months, to be dragged out, if needs be, like carcasses of meat.

"What a loathsome place!" cried Sir Charles. "Hurry up, Jack! let us get out of this, in Heaven's name!"

"Where's my man?" quickly asked Colonel Papillon in response to this appeal.

"There, the third from the left," whispered M. Floçon. "We hoped you would recognize the corpse at once."

"That? Impossible! You do not expect it, surely? Why, the face is too much mangled for any one to say who it is."

"Are there no indications, no marks or signs, to say whether it is Quadling or not?" asked the Judge in a greatly disappointed tone.

"Absolutely nothing. And yet I am quite satisfied it is not him. For the simple reason that—"

"Yes, yes, go on."

"That Quadling in person is standing out there among the crowd."

20

M. Floçon was the first to realize the full meaning of
Colonel Papillon's surprising statement.

"Run, run, La Pêche! Have the outer doors closed; let
no one leave the place."

"Draw back, gentlemen!" he went on, and he hustled
his companions with frantic haste out at the back of the
mortuary chamber. "Pray Heaven he has not seen us! He
would know us, even if we do not him."

Then with no less haste he seized Colonel Papillon by
the arm and hurried him by the back passages through
the office into the outer, public chamber, where the
astonished crowd stood, silent and perturbed, awaiting
explanation of their detention.

"Quick, monsieur!" whispered the Chief; "point him
out to me."

The request was not unnecessary, for when Colonel
Papillon went forward, and, putting his hand on a man's
shoulder, saying, "Mr. Quadling, I think," the police
officer was scarcely able to restrain his surprise.

The person thus challenged was very unlike any one
he had seen before that day, Ripaldi most of all. The
moustache was gone, the clothes were entirely changed; a
pair of dark green spectacles helped the disguise. It was
strange indeed that Papillon had known him; but at the
moment of recognition Quadling had removed his glasses,
no doubt that he might the better examine the object of
his visit to the Morgue, that gruesome record of his own
fell handiwork.

Naturally he drew back with well-feigned indignation,
muttering half-unintelligible words in French, denying

stoutly both in voice and gesture all acquaintance with
the person who thus abruptly addressed him.

"This is not to be borne," he cried. "Who are you that
dares—"

"Ta! ta!" quietly put in M. Floçon; "we will discuss
that fully, but not here. Come into the office; come, I say,
or must we use force?"

There was no escaping now, and with a poor attempt
at bravado the stranger was led away.

"Now, Colonel Papillon, look at him well. Do you know
him? Are you satisfied it is—"

"Mr. Quadling, late banker, of Rome. I have not the
slightest doubt of it. I recognize him beyond all question."

"That will do. Silence, sir!" This to Quadling. "No
observations. I too can recognize you now as the person
who called himself Ripaldi an hour or two ago. Denial is
useless. Let him be searched; thoroughly, you
understand, La Pêche? Call in your other men; he may
resist."

They gave the wretched man but scant consideration,
and in less than three minutes had visited every pocket,
examined every secret receptacle, and practically turned
him inside out.

After this there could no longer be any doubt of his
identity, still less of his complicity in the crime.

First among the many damning evidences of his guilt
was the missing pocketbook of the porter of the sleeping-
car. Within was the train card and the passengers'
tickets, all the papers which the man Groote had lost so
unaccountably. They had, of course, been stolen from his
person with the obvious intention of impeding the inquiry
into the murder. Next, in another inner pocket was
Quadling's own wallet, with his own visiting-cards,
several letters addressed to him by name; above all, a
thick sheaf of bank-notes of all nationalities—English,
French, Italian, and amounting in total value to several
thousands of pounds.

"Well, do you still deny? Bah! it is childish, useless, mere waste of breath. At last we have penetrated the mystery. You may as well confess. Whether or no, we have enough to convict you by independent testimony," said the Judge, severely. "Come, what have you to say?"

But Quadling, with pale, averted face, stood obstinately mute. He was in the toils, the net had closed round him, they should have no assistance from him.

"Come, speak out; it will be best. Remember, we have means to make you—"

"Will you interrogate him further, M. Beaumont le Hardi? Here, at once?"

"No, let him be removed to the Prefecture; it will be more convenient; to my private office."

Without more ado a fiacre was called, and the prisoner was taken off under escort, M. Floçon seated by his side, one policeman in front, another on the box, and lodged in a secret cell at the Quai l'Horloge.

"And you, gentlemen?" said the Judge to Sir Charles and Colonel Papillon. "I do not wish to detain you further, although there may be points you might help us to elucidate if I might venture to still trespass on your time?"

Sir Charles was eager to return to the Hôtel Madagascar, and yet he felt that he should best serve his dear Countess by seeing this to the end. So he readily assented to accompany the Judge, and Colonel Papillon, who was no less curious, agreed to go too.

"I sincerely trust," said the Judge on the way, "that our people have laid hands on that woman Petitpré. I believe that she holds the key to the situation, that when we hear her story we shall have a clear case against Quadling; and—who knows?—she may completely exonerate Madame la Comtesse."

During the events just recorded, which occupied a good hour, the police agents had time to go and come from the Rue Bellechasse. They did not return empty-handed, although at first it seemed as if they had made a fruitless journey. The Hôtel Ivoire was a very second-class place, a lodging-house, or hotel with furnished rooms let out by the week to lodgers with whom the proprietor had no very close acquaintance. His clerk did all the business, and this functionary produced the register, as he is bound by law, for the inspection of the police officers, but afforded little information as to the day's arrivals.

"Yes, a man calling himself Dufour had taken rooms about midday, one for himself, one for madame who was with him, also named Dufour–his sister, he said;" and he went on at the request of the police officers to describe them.

"Our birds," said the senior agent, briefly. "They are wanted. We belong to the detective police."

"All right." Such visits were not new to the clerk.

"But you will not find monsieur; he is out; there hangs his key. Madame? No, she is within. Yes, that is certain, for not long since she rang her bell. There, it goes again."

He looked up at the furiously oscillating bell, but made no move.

"Bah! they do not pay for service; let her come and say what she needs."

"Exactly; and we will bring her," said the officer, making for the stairs and the room indicated.

But on reaching the door, they found it locked. From within? Hardly, for as they stood there in doubt, a voice inside cried vehemently:

"Let me out! Help! Help! Send for the police. I have much to tell them. Quick! Let me out."

"We are here, my dear, just as you require us. But wait; step down, Gaston, and see if the clerk has a second key. If not, call in a locksmith–the nearest. A little patience only, my beauty. Do not fear."

The key was quickly produced, and an entrance effected.

A woman stood there in a defiant attitude, with arms akimbo; she, no doubt, of whom they were in search. A tall, rather masculine-looking creature, with a dark, handsome face, bold black eyes just now flashing fiercely, rage in every feature.

"Madame Dufour?" began the police officer.

"Dufour! Rot! My name is Hortense Petitpré; who are you? *La Rousse?*" (Police.)

"At your service. Have you anything to say to us? We have come on purpose to take you to the Prefecture quietly, if you will let us; or–"

"I will go quietly. I ask nothing better. I have to lay information against a miscreant–a murderer–the vile assassin who would have made me his accomplice–the banker, Quadling, of Rome!"

In the fiacre Hortense Petitpré talked on with such incessant abuse, virulent and violent, of Quadling, that her charges were neither precise nor intelligible.

It was not until she appeared before M. Beaumont le Hardi, and was handled with great dexterity by that practised examiner, that her story took definite form.

What she had to say will be best told in the clear, formal language of the official disposition.

The witness inculpated stated:

"She was named Aglaé Hortense Petitpré, thirty-four years of age, a Frenchwoman, born in Paris, Rue de Vincennes No. 374. Was engaged by the Contessa Castagneto, November 19, 189–, in Rome, as lady's maid, and there, at her mistress's domicile, became acquainted with the Sieur Francis Quadling, a banker of the Via Condotti, Rome.

"Quadling had pretensions to the hand of the Countess, and sought, by bribes and entreaties, to interest witness in his suit. Witness often spoke of him in complimentary terms to her mistress, who was not very favourably disposed towards him.

"One afternoon (two days before the murder) Quadling paid a lengthened visit to the Countess. Witness did not hear what occurred, but Quadling came out much distressed, and again urged her to speak to the Countess. He had heard of the approaching departure of the lady from Rome, but said nothing of his own intentions.

"Witness was much surprised to find him in the sleeping-car, but had no talk to him till the following morning, when he asked her to obtain an interview for him with the Countess, and promised a large reward. In making this offer he produced a wallet and exhibited a very large number of notes.

"Witness was unable to persuade the Countess, although she returned to the subject frequently. Witness so informed Quadling, who then spoke to the lady, but was coldly received.

"During the journey witness thought much over the situation. Admitted that the sight of Quadling's money had greatly disturbed her, but, although pressed, would not say when the first idea of robbing him took possession of her. (Note by Judge—That she had resolved to do so is, however, perfectly clear, and the conclusion is borne out by her acts. It was she who secured the Countess's medicine bottle; she, beyond doubt, who drugged the porter at Laroche. In no other way can her presence in the sleeping-car between Laroche and Paris be accounted for-presence which she does not deny.)

"Witness at last reluctantly confessed that she entered the compartment where the murder was committed, and at a critical moment. An affray was actually in progress between the Italian Ripaldi and the incriminated man Quadling, but the witness arrived as the last fatal blow was struck by the latter.

"She saw it struck, and saw the victim fall lifeless on the floor.

"Witness declared she was so terrified she could at first utter no cry, nor call for help, and before she could recover herself the murderer threatened her with the ensanguined knife. She threw herself on her knees, imploring pity, but the man Quadling told her that she was an eye-witness, and could take him to the guillotine,—she also must die.

"Witness at last prevailed on him to spare her life, but only on condition that she would leave the car. He indicated the window as the only way of escape; but on this for a long time she refused to venture, declaring that it was only to exchange one form of death for another. Then, as Quadling again threatened to stab her, she was compelled to accept this last chance, never hoping to win out alive.

"With Quadling's assistance, however, she succeeded in climbing out through the window and in gaining the roof. He had told her to wait for the first occasion when the train slackened speed to leave it and shift for herself. With this intention he gave her a thousand francs, and bade her never show herself again.

"Witness descended from the train not far from the small station of Villeneuve on the line, and there took the local train for Paris. Landed at the Lyons Station, she heard of the inquiry in progress, and then, waiting outside, saw Quadling disguised as the Italian leave in company with another man. She followed and marked Quadling down, meaning to denounce him on the first opportunity. Quadling, however, on issuing from the restaurant, had accosted her, and at once offered her a further sum of five thousand francs as the price of silence, and she had gone with him to the Hôtel Ivoire, where she was to receive the sum. Quadling had paid it, but on one condition, that she would remain at the Hotel Ivoire until the following day. Apparently he had distrusted her, for he had contrived to lock her into her compartment. As she did not choose to be so imprisoned, she summoned assistance, and was at length released by the police."

This was the substance of Hortense Petitpré's deposition, and it was corroborated in many small details.

When she appeared before the Judge, with whom Sir Charles Collingham and Colonel Papillon were seated, the former at once pointed out that she was wearing a dark mantle trimmed with the same sort of passementerie as that picked up in the sleeping-car.

L'Envoi .

Quadling was in due course brought before the Court of Assize and tried for his life. There was no sort of doubt of his guilt, and the jury so found, but, having regard to certain extenuating circumstances, they recommended him to mercy. The chief of these was Quadling's positive assurance that he had been first attacked by Ripaldi; he declared that the Italian detective had in the first instance tried to come to terms with him, demanding 50,000 francs as his price for allowing him to go at large; that when Quadling distinctly refused to be black-mailed, Ripaldi struck at him with a knife, but that the blow failed to take effect.

Then Quadling closed with him and took the knife from him. It was a fierce encounter, and might have ended either way, but the unexpected entrance of the woman Petitpré took off Ripaldi's attention, and then he, Quadling, maddened and reckless, stabbed him to the heart.

It was not until after the deed was done that Quadling realized the full measure of his crime and its inevitable consequences. Then, in a daring effort to extricate himself, he intimidated the woman Petitpré, and forced her to escape through the sleeping-car window.

It was he who had rung the signal-bell to stop the train and give her a chance of leaving it. It was after the murder, too, that he conceived the idea of personating Ripaldi, and, having disfigured him beyond recognition, as he hoped, he had changed clothes and compartments.

On the strength of this confession Quadling escaped the guillotine, but he was transported to New Caledonia for life.

The money taken on him was forwarded to Rome, and was usefully employed in reducing his liabilities to the depositors in the bank.

The other word.

Sometime in June the following announcement appeared in all the Paris papers:

"Yesterday, at the British Embassy, General Sir Charles Collingham, K. C. B., was married to Sabine, Contessa di Castagneto, widow of the Italian Count of that name."

Now from the Resurrected Press

The Hampstead Mystery

High Court Justice Sir Horace Fewbanks found shot dead in his Hampstead home, a butler with a criminal past, a scorned lover and a hint of scandal. These are the elements of the *Hampstead Mystery* that Detective Inspector Chippenfield of Scotland Yard must unravel with the assistance of the ambitious Detective Rolfe. But will he be able to sort out the tangled threads of this case and arrest the culprit before he is upstaged by the celebrated gentleman detective Crewe. Follow the details of this amazing case at it plays out across Hampstead, London and Scotland until it reaches a stunning conclusion in the courts of the Old Bailey.

The Hampstead Mystery
by John R. Watson & Arthur J. Rees
RPM -101

Visit www.resurrectedpress.com to order now.

Other Resurrected Press Mysteries

From the pen of R. Austin Freeman

Dr. John Thorndyke - Lecturer on Medical Jurisprudence and Forensic Medicine. Before Bones, before CSI, before Quincy, M.E – there was Dr. John Thorndyke solving the most baffling cases of Edwardian London using the latest tools of medical science. Read about his cases in:

The Eye of Osiris
John Bellingham, noted Egyptologist has vanished not once but twice in the same day. Now Dr, Thorndyke must unravel the tangled claims on his estate, solve the riddle of the missing man and find the "Eye of Osiris".

The Mystery of 31 New Inn
When Dr. Jervis is whisked away in a coach with no windows to an unknown location to treat a man in a coma from undivulged causes it is Dr. Thorndyke who must come up with the solution.

The Red Thumb Mark
The first of Dr. Thorndyke's cases finds him trying to prove the innocence of a young man accused of being a diamond thief despite the fact that his finger print was found at the scene of the crime.

John Thorndyke's Cases
More cases of medical mysteries as told by his trusted assistant Jervis, M.D. Eight stories of crime and deduction in Edwardian London.

Visit www.resurrectedpress.com

The Fictional Detective
by Greg Fowlkes

Who killed Ezekial O. Handler?

A beautiful dame, a hard-boiled private eye – and a dead body.

It started like any other case. When a famous writer dies in a mysterious car crash, private detective Frank Slade is called in to find answers, but all he finds is more questions. Who killed Ezekial Handler? Who is Janet Nielsen and why is she so interested in finding out? Who is leaving the neatly typed clues? And as Slade tries to find answers to these questions he starts to wonder if the ultimate answer will threaten his very existence.

Read about it in
The Fictional Detective

Visit www.thefictionaldetective.com

About Resurrected Press

A division of Intrepid Ink, LLC, Resurrected Press is dedicated to bringing high quality, vintage books back into publication. See our entire catalogue and find out more at www.ResurrectedPress.com.

About Intrepid Ink, LLC

Intrepid Ink, LLC provides full publishing services to authors of fiction and non-fiction books, eBooks and websites. From editing to formatting, from publishing to marketing, Intrepid Ink gets your creative works into the hands of the people who want to read them. Find out more at www.IntrepidInk.com.